Escape
from Shangri-La

Escape
from Shangri-La

MICHAEL MORPURGO

EGMONT

For Conrad and Anne

EGMONT

We bring stories to life

The extract (p76) of 'Little Gidding' from *Four Quartets*,
Collected Poems 1909-1962 by T.S. Eliot is reproduced by permission
of Faber and Faber Limited.

First published in Great Britain in 1998 by Heinemann Young Books
This edition published 2011 by Egmont UK Limited
239 Kensington High Street London W8 6SA

Text copyright © 1998 Michael Morpurgo
Cover images © 2011 Shutterstock

The moral rights of the author have been asserted

ISBN 978 1 4052 2670 7

9 10 8

A CIP catalogue record for this title is available from the
British Library

Printed and bound in Great Britain by the CPI Group

35223/13

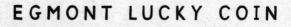

EGMONT LUCKY COIN

Our story began over a century ago, when seventeen-year-old
Egmont Harald Petersen found a coin in the street.

He was on his way to buy a flyswatter, a small hand-operated
printing machine that he then set up in his tiny apartment.

The coin brought him such good luck that today Egmont has
offices in over 30 countries around the world. And that lucky
coin is still kept at the company's head offices in Denmark.

CONTENTS

1	A bit of old goat	1
2	Water music	12
3	Barnardo's boys	25
4	The prodigal father	37
5	Nowhere man	51
6	And all shall be well	64
7	Shangri-La	79
8	The *Lucie Alice*	95
9	Gone missing	113
10	Dunkirk	134
11	The great escape	158
12	Earlie in the morning	177
13	Message to my father	195

1 A BIT OF AN OLD GOAT

I WAS KNEELING UP AGAINST THE BACK OF THE sofa looking out of the window. Summer holidays and raining, raining streams. 'He's been there all day,' I said.

'Who has?' My mother was still doing the ironing. 'I don't know why,' she went on, 'but I love ironing. Therapeutic, restorative, satisfying. Not like teaching at all. Teaching's definitely not therapeutic.' She talked a lot about teaching, even in the holidays.

'That man. He just stands there. He just stands there staring at us.'

'It's a free world, isn't it?'

The old man was standing on the opposite side of the road outside Mrs Martin's house underneath the lamppost. Sometimes he'd be leaning up against it, and sometimes he'd be just standing there, shoulders hunched, his hands deep in his pockets. But always he'd be looking, looking right at me. He was wearing a blue donkey jacket – or perhaps it was a sailor's jacket, I couldn't tell – the collar turned up against the rain. His hair was long, long and white, and it seemed to be tied up in a ponytail behind him. He looked like some ancient Viking warlord.

'Come and see,' I said. 'He's strange, really strange.' But she never even looked up. How anyone could be so obsessively absorbed in ironing was beyond me. She was patting the shirt she'd finished, sadly, her head on one side, just as if she was saying goodbye to an old dog. I turned to the window again.

'What's he up to? He must be soaked. Mum!' At last she came over. She was kneeling beside me on the sofa now and smelling all freshly ironed herself. 'All day, he's been there all day, ever since breakfast. Honest.'

'All that hair,' she tutted. 'He looks a bit of a tramp if you ask me, a bit of an old goat.' And she wrinkled up her nose in disapproval, as if she could smell him, even from this far away.

'And what's wrong with tramps, then?' I said. 'I thought you said it was a free world.'

'Free-ish, Cessie dear, only free-ish.' And she leant across me and closed the curtains. 'There, now he can

2

look at the back of our William Morris lily pattern to his heart's content, and we don't have to look at him any more, do we?' She smiled her ever so knowing smile at me. 'Do you think I was born yesterday, Cessie Stevens? Do you think I don't know what this is all about? It's the "p" word, isn't it? Pro . . . cras . . . tin . . . ation.' She was right of course. She enunciated it excruciatingly slowly, deliberately teasing the word out for greatest effect. She was expert at it. My mother wasn't a teacher for nothing. 'Violin practice, Cessie. First you said you'd do it this morning, then you were going to do it this afternoon. And now it's already this evening and you still haven't done it, have you?'

She was off the sofa now and crouching down in front of me, looking into my face, her hands on mine. 'Come on. Before your dad gets home. You know how it upsets him when you don't practise. Be an angel.'

'I am not an angel,' I said firmly. 'And I don't want to be an angel either.' I was out of the room and up the stairs before she could say another word.

I was ambivalent about my mother. I was closer to her than anyone else in this world. She had always been my only confidant, my most trusted friend. Whatever I did, she would always defend me to the hilt. I'd overhear her talking about me. 'She's just going through that awkward prickly stage,' she'd explain. 'Half girl, half woman. Not the one thing, nor the other. She'll come out of it.' But sometimes she just couldn't stop playing teacher. Worst of all, she would use my father as a weapon against me. In fact, my father was never really upset when I didn't practise my violin, but I knew that he would be disappointed. And I hated to disappoint him – she knew that too.

Whenever he could, whenever he was home, my father would come up to my room to hear me play. He'd sit back in my chair, put his hands behind his head and close his eyes. When I played well – and I usually did when he was there – he would give me a huge bear hug afterwards, and say something like, 'Eat your heart out, Yehudi.' But just recently, ever since we moved house, my father hadn't been able to hear me that much. His new job at the radio station kept him busier than ever – he had two shows a day and some at weekends too. I'd listen in from time to time just to hear his voice, but it was never the same. He was never my father on the radio.

I was ambivalent about my violin too. The truth was that I loved it with a passion. I loved the secrecy of its hidden life shut away in its green baize case, the soft snuggle of the pad under my chin, the smoothness of the horsehair when I drew my bow across the inside of my wrist to test its tautness. I loved playing my violin too, but I had always hated practising, and in particular I hated being told to practise. Once I could forget that I was practising, once I could lose myself in the music, then I could play quite happily for hours on end and not even notice the passing of time.

I was just beginning to enjoy it, just beginning to feel at one with my violin. I was playing Handel's *Largo* so well I could feel my skin pricking with pleasure all down my arms. But then the doorbell rang. The magic was broken. I was immediately back to hateful practising. The bell rang again. Any excuse to avoid practising was good enough. I put the violin down on my bed, and my bow too, and went to the top of the stairs to see who it was. I heard the front door opening. There was a shadow down in the hallway, and my mother was standing beside it, motionless.

'Who is it?' I said, as I came down the stairs.

The shadow moved suddenly into the light of the hallway and became the old man from across the road. He was standing there, dripping. 'I'm sorry,' he said. 'I don't want to intrude.'

His face tremored into a smile as he saw me. 'Cessie?' He knew my name! 'You must be Cessie. I know this is going to sound a bit odd, but I'm your grandad. I'm your dad's dad, so that makes me your grandad, doesn't it?' He looked full at my mother now. 'It's true, true as I'm standing here. I'm young Arthur's dad. When I knew him last he was only little, five years old, and that's near enough fifty years ago. Long time.' For a moment or two, he didn't seem to know what else to say. 'Big ears. Born with big ears, he was, like a baby elephant. That's why we called him Arthur. You know those Babar books, do you?' I nodded because I couldn't speak. 'I was Babar, if you see what I mean. His mum was Celeste, and so the little fellow, our son, was called Arthur. He didn't have a trunk of course.' I smiled at that, and he caught it and tossed it back at me, his eyes suddenly bright.

'You'd be a bit old for all that now, I suppose. All grown up, I expect.' He was scrutinising me now. 'Come to think of it, you look a bit like little Arthur too, except for the ears of course. You've got nice ears, nice and neat, like they should be. Not flapping around in the wind like his were. What are you? Thirteen? Fourteen?'

'Eleven,' I said. I felt my mother take my hand and hold on to it tightly, so tightly it was hurting me.

'Seventy-five.' The old man was pointing to himself. 'I'm seventy-five. Old as the hills, eh? Do you know what your dad used to call me when he was little? "Popsicle". "Pops" to start off with. Then it was Popsicle. Don't know why. It's what everyone's always called me ever since – Popsicle, Popsicle Stevens.'

'You can't be,' my mother whispered, pulling me close to her. 'You can't be him. Arthur hasn't got a father.' The old man seemed suddenly unsteady on his feet. He swayed and staggered forward. Instinctively we both backed away from him. He was dripping from his ears, from his chin, from his fingers too. It was as if his whole body was weeping tears. His hair, I noticed, wasn't really white at all, but creamy, almost yellow in places. It didn't look very clean. None of him did.

'Everyone's got a father,' he said, and he was holding out his arms towards us – just like ghosts do, I thought. 'I'm not a ghost, Cessie.' We backed further away. Ghosts can read minds. 'I'm telling you, I'm Popsicle Stevens and I'm Arthur's father, and I'm alive, alive, oh. I mean ghosts don't get hungry, do they? And they don't get fruzzed either.' He reached out suddenly and caught me by my wrist. 'Feel that?' He was as cold as stone, but he was real. He was no ghost. 'You wouldn't have a nice cup of tea, would you, just to warm a fellow through?'

My mother stood her ground now, pulling me behind her, clasping my hand even tighter still. 'How do

I know? You could be anyone, couldn't you? Coming in off the street like that, you could be anyone. How do I know you're who you say you are?'

The old man took a deep breath before he spoke. 'Listen, these old grey cells up here' – he was tapping his temple – 'they may not be what they once were, but there's some things you don't get wrong. If you've got an Arthur Stevens living here, and he grew up in a little place called Bradwell-on-Sea – on the Essex coast it is – if he's your husband, and if he's your dad, then, unless I'm mistaken – which I don't think I am – we're kith and kin, all of us. I just thought I'd look him up, that's all. I didn't think it could do any harm – not now, not any more.'

In the silence of the hallway I could almost hear my mother thinking, perhaps because we were thinking the same thing. My father *had* grown up on the Essex coast. We'd been there. We'd seen the house where he was born. His childhood was a bit of a mystery. He'd been a Barnado's boy – I knew that much. His mother, my grandmother, had died young – I knew that too – a long time before I was born. As for his father, I'd known little or nothing of him. My father had never spoken of him, not in my hearing anyway. If I had thought about him at all, and I am not sure that I had, then I

8

suppose I had simply presumed he was dead, like my grandmother was.

The old man was unbuttoning his jacket now, and fumbling deep inside. My mother still held me by the hand in a grip of steel. The wallet he took out was stuffed full, like some battered leather sandwich. He opened it up with great care, almost reverently. With shaky fingers he pulled out an old photograph, faded to sepia, torn at the edges and criss-crossed with creases. He gave it to us. A young man looked at me out of the photograph. He was standing in front of a clapperboard house with roses growing up around the windows. Astride his shoulders sat a small boy clutching his hair with both fists. Beside them stood a young woman who was looking up at them adoringly.

'That's your grandmother,' he said, 'and there's me with little Arthur, your dad, that is, pulling my hair by the roots. He was always doing that, little rascal. Summer 1950. That was the last summer we were all together.'

'What was she called?' My mother was still interrogating him. 'Arthur's mother. What was she called?'

The question clearly troubled him. He seemed reluctant to answer, but when he spoke at last he spoke very deliberately. 'Cecilia,' he said. 'She was called Cecilia.' Then he was looking at me and beaming. 'Of course. I didn't think of it till now, Cessie. That'd be after your grandmother, wouldn't it?'

He was right. He'd been right about everything. I felt a warm shiver creeping up the back of my neck. My grandmother *had* been called Cecilia, and I *had* been named after her, I'd always known that. There was a photograph of her on top of the piano in the sitting-room. She was young in the photograph, somehow too young for me to have ever thought of her as a grandmother.

I looked up into his face. The eyes were deep-set and gentle. They were blue. He had blue eyes. My father had blue eyes. I had blue eyes. That was the moment the last doubts vanished. This man had to be my father's father, my grandfather.

For some time we just stood there and stared at him.

I squeezed my mother's hand, urging her to do something, say something, anything. She looked down at me. I could see she was still unsure. But I knew he was not lying. I knew what lying was all about. I did it a lot. This man was not doing it. It takes a liar to know a liar.

'You'd better come in,' I said.

I broke free of my mother's grasp, took my grandfather gently by the arm and led him into the warmth of the kitchen.

2 WATER MUSIC

'I'M AFRAID I'VE GOT A VERY SWEET TOOTH,' HE said, stirring five heaped teaspoons of sugar into his tea. We sat watching him as he sipped and slurped, both hands holding the mug. He was savouring it. In between sips he set about the plate of chocolate digestive biscuits, dunking every one till it was soggy all through, and devouring one after another with scarcely a pause for breath. He must have been really famished. His face was weathered brown and crinkled and craggy, like the bark of an old oak tree. I'd never seen a face like it. I couldn't take my eyes off him.

I did all the talking. Someone had to. I can't stand silences – they make me uncomfortable. He was obviously too intent on his tea and biscuits to say anything at all, and my mother just sat there staring across the kitchen table at him. How many times had she told me not to stare at people? And here she was gawping at him shamelessly. It was as if Quasimodo had dropped in for tea.

I had to think of something sensible to talk about, and I reasoned that he might want to know something about me, about his new-found granddaughter. After all, he had my whole life to catch up on. So I gave him a potted autobiography, heavily selective, just the bits I thought might be interesting: how we'd just moved here six months ago, where I went to school, who my worst enemies were. I told him in particular about Shirley Watson and Mandy Bethel, and about how they'd always baited me at school, because I was new perhaps, or maybe because I kept myself to myself and was never one of the girls. All the while he kept on chomping and slurping, but he was listening too. I could tell he was because he was smiling at all the right places. I'd told him just about everything I could think of, when I remembered my violin.

'I'm Grade Five now. I started when I was three, didn't I, Mum? Suzuki method. I do two lessons a week with Madame Poitou – she's French and she's a lot better than my old teacher. She says I've got a good ear, but I'm a bit lazy. I have to practise every day for forty minutes. Not much good at anything else, except swimming. Butterfly, I'm really good at butterfly. Oh, yes, and I like sailing too. Dad's got a friend who works at the radio station with him, and he's got a twenty-six footer called *Seaventure*. He keeps it down at the marina. We went all the way down the coast, didn't we, Mum? Dartmouth or somewhere. Bit rough, but it was great.'

'Nothing like it,' he said, nodding away. 'Nothing like the sea. "I must go down to the sea again, to the lonely sea and the sky . . ." you know that poem, do you? Not true, of course. You're never lonely at sea. It's people that make you feel lonely, don't you think? You like poetry, do you? Always liked poems, I have. I've got dozens of them up here in my head.'

My mother spoke up suddenly: 'How did you know where to find us? How did you know?'

'It was luck, just luck. It wasn't as if I was looking for him. It just happened. I was at home, a couple of weeks ago, and I had the radio on. Had it on for the weather, matter of fact. I always listen to the weather. I heard him, on that programme he does in the mornings. I didn't recognise his voice of course, but there was something about how he said what he said that I had to listen to. And then I heard his name. "Arthur Stevens'

Morning Chat", they called it. I'm not a fool. I knew well enough there was likely to be more than one Arthur Stevens in the world, I knew that. But I just had this feeling, like it was a meant-to-be thing. Do you understand what I'm saying? It was like we were supposed to meet up again after all this time.

'So, the same afternoon it was, I went and had a look. I walked right in the front door of the radio station. And there he was, larger than life up on the wall, a huge great smiling poster of him. I took one look and, I'm telling you, I didn't have to read the signature across the bottom. It was him. Same big ears, same cheeky smile, same little Arthur. Just fifty years older, that's all. Couldn't mistake him. And then, whilst I was standing there looking up at him, he comes right past me, close enough I could've reached out and touched him. And I wanted to, believe me I wanted to; but I couldn't, I didn't dare. Then he was gone out of the door and it was too late.'

He swept the biscuit crumbs up into a little pile with his finger, and went on. 'Anyway, after that I came over all giddy in the head. I get that from time to time. I had to sit down to steady myself, and there was this young lady at the desk who helped me. She was nice too. She brought me a glass of water. I reckon she was a bit worried about me. After a bit, we got talking, her and me. I asked her about Arthur and she told me all about him – and about the two of you as well. She said how good he is to work with, how he cares about what he does. "Never stops," she said. "Works himself to a frazzle." She told me about all the shows he does, how they phone in with all their cares and woes, and how he talks to them and makes them feel better about themselves. "You should listen in some time," she said. So I did. I've heard every one of his pro- grammes ever since – never missed. Not once. Plays my kind of music too.'

He was looking at us hard. 'I know what you're thinking. You're thinking I'm maybe a bit crazed in the head, a bit barmy. Well, maybe I am at that. Maybe I shouldn't have come at all. I've got no business being here, I suppose, not really, not after all these years.' His eyes were welling with tears. 'It was an agreement, a sort of understanding, between Arthur's mother and me. Don't get me wrong. I don't blame her – I wasn't much good to her, I know that now. One day she just said she'd had enough. She was leaving and she was taking young Arthur with her. She wanted a fresh start, she said. There was this other man – these things happen. Anyway it wasn't nasty, nothing like that. It'd be best all round if I stayed out of it, she said, best for the boy. He'd soon get used to a new father. So I said I'd keep away, for the boy's sake. And that's what I've done. I kept my promise, and it wasn't easy sometimes, I can tell you. A father always wants to know how his son's grown up. So I never went looking; but when I heard his name on the radio, well, like I said, I thought it was a meant thing. And here I am. He sounded grand on the radio, just grand.' He brushed away the tears with the back of his hand. He had massively broad hands, brown and engrained with dirt. 'It took me two weeks thinking about it, and then a whole day standing out there in the rain before I could bring myself to knock on the door.'

He composed himself again before he went on. He was looking directly at my mother. 'I haven't come to bother you, nor him. I promise. I just wanted to see him, see you all, and then I'll be on my way.'

My mother glanced up at the kitchen clock. 'Well, I'm afraid he's not going to be home for quite a while yet. Half an hour at least, maybe longer.' Then, quite suddenly, she snapped into teacher mode again – positive, confident, organising. 'All right,' she said. 'Cessie, you can go and run a bath.'

'What?' Sometimes I just could not understand her

at all. Why on earth should I have a bath all of a sudden, and before supper too?

'Not for you, Cessie, for Mr Stevens.' She clapped her hands at me. 'Go on, hop to it. And he'll need a towel too, from the airing cupboard – the big green one. We can't have Mr Stevens sitting around in those wet clothes till your father comes home, can we now? He'll catch his death.'

'Not Mr Stevens, please. Popsicle. I'm Popsicle,' my grandfather said quietly. 'I'd like it very much if you'd call me Popsicle. It's what everyone calls me. It's what I'm used to.'

My mother had been interrupted in full flow, but she was only momentarily taken aback. 'Popsicle it is then,' she said, and she bustled me out of the kitchen. 'I'll look out some of Arthur's clothes for you,' I heard her telling him as I went up the stairs. 'They'll be a bit on the large side, I shouldn't wonder. We'll have those wet things of yours dry in a jiffy.' She was talking to him as if she'd known him for years, as if he was one of the family.

I was thinking about that as I ran the bath, but it wasn't until I was fetching the towel from the airing cupboard that it began to sink in, that I began to under-stand what all this really meant. Until then I had believed it, but I hadn't felt it. I had a new grandfather. Out of nowhere I had a new grandfather! A flush of sudden joy surged through me. As I watched him coming slowly up the stairs, hauling himself up by the banisters, all I wanted to do was to throw my arms round his neck and hug him. I waited until he reached the top, and then I did it. He looked a bit bewildered. I'd taken him by surprise but I think he was pleased all the same.

'Do you have a loofah, Cessie?' he asked me. 'I don't have baths very often. Bit difficult where I live. Bit cramped. Never enough water either. But when I do have a bath I always have my loofah.'

'What's that?' I asked.

'It's a sort of backscrubber. Reaches the parts you can't reach otherwise.'

'I don't think we've got one,' I laughed. 'But you can have a duck, if you want. I've got a yellow plastic one called Patsy. Had it ever since I was little.'

'What more could a fellow want?' He smiled at me as I handed him the towel. 'Tell you what, Cessie, why don't you give us a tune on that fiddle of yours, eh? Same tune you were playing when I was out in the street. I liked that. I liked that a lot. You could do me a sort of serenade in the bath.'

So, with my bedroom door open, I serenaded him with Handel's *Largo*. I could hear him humming away and splashing next door in the bathroom. I was playing so well, I was so wrapped up in it, that at first I didn't notice my mother standing at the door of my room. I could tell she'd been listening for some time. When I stopped playing she said, 'You play so well, Cessie. When you mean it, you play so well.' She came over and sat down on my bed. 'I don't know what it is. I don't feel right in myself,' she said. 'Shock, I suppose. I can't explain it. It's like someone's just walked over my grave.' I sat down beside her. She seemed to want me to. 'It *is* him, you know,' she went on. 'I can see your dad in his face, in his gestures. You can't fake that.' She was hugging herself. 'Maybe I'm frightened, Cessie.'

'Of him?'

'No, of course not. Of what might happen when your dad gets back. I don't understand. I just don't know what to make of it. I mean he'll talk occasionally about his mum, and, very occasionally, about his stepfather too. But in all the time I've known him I don't think he's ever said a single word to me about his real dad. It's as if he never existed, like he was almost a non-person. Perhaps I should have asked, but I always felt it was . . .

well . . . like forbidden territory, almost as if there was something to hide, something he didn't want to remember. I don't know, I don't know; but what I do know is that any minute now your dad's going to walk in this house, and I'm going to have to tell him his father's here. It's going to be a big surprise, but I'm not sure what kind of surprise, that's all.'

'I'll tell him, if you like,' I said. I didn't make the offer just to help her out. I offered because I wanted to be quite sure I was there when he was told, that this wouldn't be one of those private, important things they went out into the garden to discuss earnestly. Popsicle may be my father's father, but when all was said and done, he was my grandfather not theirs.

My mother put her hand on mine. 'We'll do it together, shall we?'

That was the moment we heard the front door open, and then slam. My father always slammed the door. It was part of his homecoming ritual. He'd toss the car keys next.

'Anyone home?' We heard the car keys land on the hall table. He was walking into the kitchen. 'Anyone home?'

I don't know who was squeezing whose hand the harder as we walked together along the landing past the bathroom door. We went down the stairs side by side, holding hands, and into the kitchen, holding hands. My father had his back to us. He was by the sink pouring himself a can of beer. He turned round and took a couple of deep swigs. I had never noticed how big his ears were, but I noticed now. I had to smile in spite of myself. My mother was right. You could see Popsicle in him. He was younger of course, and without the long, yellow hair, but they were so alike.

He smothered a burp and patted his chest. 'Pardon me,' he said. 'Throat's as dry as a bone.'

'It's all that talking you do,' my mother said, clearing her throat nervously.

'What's up?' He was looking at us, from one to the other. We looked back. 'Nothing the matter, is there? You all right, Cessie?' I looked away.

My mother began clearing the table, busily. She wasn't a very convincing actress. 'So,' she said, 'so you won't be wanting a cup of tea then, not after a beer.'

My father was looking down at the kitchen table. He was counting the mugs, I was sure of it. 'Seems like tea's over and done with anyway. You been having a party, have you?' I smiled weakly. I could think of nothing to say.

'Cessie's done her violin practice.' My mother was prattling now. 'And I have to say that she's playing the *Largo* quite beautifully.' She was bent over the table, wiping it down, but with far too much enthusiasm. As I watched her I could see she was never going to be able to bring herself even to look at him, let alone to break the news. I was bursting to tell him, but I didn't know how to begin. I couldn't find the words. I couldn't just blurt it out, could I? I couldn't say: 'Your long lost father's come back to see you. He's upstairs having a bath, with Patsy.'

I was still trying to work out how to tell him, when we heard the bathroom door open, and slow, heavy footfalls coming down the stairs.

'Who's that?' My father had put down his beer. He knew now for sure that there was some sort of conspiracy going on.

'Are you in there? Are you in the kitchen?' Popsicle was talking all the time as he came down the stairs, as he came across the hallway towards the kitchen. 'The clothes are fine. Jacket's bit big in the sleeve. I may look like a right old scarecrow, but at least I'm a clean old scarecrow now, and warm too. Warmed right through, I am. Best bath I've had in years. And it's been a very long time, I can tell you, since I had a bath with a duck.

23

Friendly sort of a duck too, never leaves you alone. Always nibbling at something.'

The kitchen door opened. My father looked at his father. My grandfather looked at his son.

3 BARNARDO'S BOYS

POPSICLE SHUFFLED FORWARD, HESITANTLY, offering his hand as he came, but my father didn't take it, not at first. Even when he did, it was obvious to me that he had little idea whose hand he was shaking. But he knew he should know. He wanted help. He needed someone to tell him who this was. So I told him.

'He's your dad.' I said it straight out. It seemed the only way.

'You don't recognise me, do you, Arthur?' Popsicle held on to my father's hand for a moment longer. 'Why should you? Been fifty years, near enough. Last time I saw you was in Bradwell, in the village. You were catching a bus across the road from the church, a green bus, I remember that. You and your mum were off to live in Maldon, just down the coast. You were looking out the back window and you were waving. Never saw you again after that, nor your mum.'

Still my father said nothing. He seemed to be in some kind of a trance, incapable of movement, incapable of speech. I had never seen him like this and it frightened me.

My mother was trying to explain. 'He heard you on the radio, Arthur,' she said. 'And then he went to the radio station. He saw your picture on the wall. Recognised you right away, didn't you, Popsicle?'

'Bradwell-on-Sea?' My father spoke at last.

Popsicle nodded. 'Remember the house, do you, Arthur? Down by the quay, next to the Green Man. Good pub that. Too good.'

My father said nothing more. The silence was becoming long and awkward. I suppose I had been anticipating a joyous reunion, huge hugs, tears even. I certainly hadn't expected this. My father was usually so spontaneous. This wasn't like him at all.

'Maybe I shouldn't have come, Arthur,' said Popsicle at last. 'Not without warning you anyway. I should have written a letter perhaps. That would've been better. Well, maybe I'd better be off then.' And he turned away towards the door.

'You'll do no such thing,' said my mother firmly. She

had Popsicle by the arm now. 'No one's going anywhere. If this man is who he says he is, then there's more than just the two of you involved in this. There's Cessie and there's me.' She sat Popsicle down on a kitchen chair, none too gently. Then she stood behind him, hands on his shoulders, facing my father.

'Well, Arthur, we need to know. Is this your father, or isn't it?'

My father took his time before replying. 'Yes.' He spoke softly, so softly I could hardly hear him. 'I remember the bus. The window was steamed up and I had to rub a hole in it to see him. I wasn't waving, not exactly.'

'Maybe Cessie and I should just leave you both alone for a while. There'll be a fair bit you want to talk about, I shouldn't wonder. We'll make ourselves scarce. Come along, Cessie.'

I was reluctant to go, but it looked as if I had no choice. I was being ushered out of the door when my father called us back.

'Don't go,' he said, and he said it in such a way that I knew he needed us.

My mother was the life and soul of that first gathering around the kitchen table. She brought out the sloe gin. 'Only for very special occasions, very special people,' she said, opening the bottle. 'Five years old.

Should be perfect. Not every day a father turns up out of the blue.'

'Nor a grandfather,' I added. I was allowed a taste, but that was all. Popsicle emptied his glass in one gulp and declared that it was 'beautiful'. My father was watching him, scrutinising him all the while, but it was a long time before he said anything.

'I went back, you know.' My father spoke up suddenly. He was looking into his glass. He still hadn't touched a drop.

'Back where?' Popsicle asked.

'Bradwell. To our house.'

'What for?'

'I went looking for you. After Mum died, I ran off. But you weren't there. I asked in the pub, but you'd gone, years before, they said.'

'She's dead, Arthur? Your mum's dead?'

'A long time ago,' said my father.

'I never knew, Arthur. Honest to God, I never knew.' His face seemed suddenly very sunken and exhausted. 'When? How?'

'I was ten. Boating accident. They were both drowned, her and Bill. No one knows what happened, not really. They looked for you. Well, they told me they did anyway, but no one could find you. They packed me off to a home, a children's home. Nothing else they could do, I suppose. That's when I ran off back to Bradwell. They caught me of course. Brought me back. A Dr Barnardo's place it was, by the sea. Wasn't home exactly, but it wasn't too bad.' He took a sip of sloe gin, and then, looking directly across the table at Popsicle, he went on: 'Do you know what I'd do sometimes? Summer evenings, I'd sit on the brick wall by the gate and wait for you. I really thought that one day you'd come back and take me away. I was sure of it.'

Popsicle seemed suddenly breathless. He clutched at the table for support. 'You all right?' my mother asked, crouching down beside him.

'I'm fine, fine,' said Popsicle.

'Sure?'

Popsicle put a hand to his neck. 'There's a thing,' he said. 'Be funny if it weren't so sad. Runs in the family. Father and son, both of us Barnardo's boys. There's a thing, there's a thing.'

Without any warning at all he slumped forward off the chair. His head smashed against the corner of the table and hit the floor at my feet with a sickening, hollow crack. There was blood at once.

I had always longed to be in an ambulance on an emergency dash to hospital. When I'd twisted my ankle

I'd gone by car and there had been no drama at all, no excitement. But with Popsicle it was the real thing. The ambulance arrived at the house, lights flashing, sirens wailing. Green-overalled paramedics came dashing into the house. They were struggling to save a life under my very eyes.

As he lay there, crumpled on the kitchen floor, all the colour drained from his face, Popsicle looked very dead. I couldn't detect any sign of breathing. And there was so much blood. The paramedics felt him, listened to him, injected him and put a mask on his face. They told us again and again not to worry, that everything would be all right.

They stretchered him out to the waiting ambulance, where the radio was crackling with messages, and around which a dozen or more of our neighbours were gathered. Mandy Bethel was there, Shirley Watson's scandal-mongering sidekick from school, so I knew the news would be all over the estate in no time. Mr Goldsmith from next door was there too. And Mrs Martin from across the road, who'd hardly even spoken to me before, put her arm round my shoulder and asked me who it was that was ill. 'My grandfather,' I said, and I said it very proudly, and very loudly too, so that everyone should hear.

Then we all climbed into the ambulance with him and we were driven away at speed, sirens wailing. I only wished they hadn't closed the doors, because I should have liked to have seen their faces for a little longer, especially Mandy Bethel's. I felt suddenly very important, very much at the centre of things.

It was only when I was inside the ambulance and looking down at Popsicle, deathly white under the scarlet of the blanket, that I realised this was not a performance at all. Suddenly it was serious and I could think only that I didn't want Popsicle to die. I didn't say prayers all that often, only when I really needed to. I needed to now, badly. I had just found myself a grandfather, or he had found me, and I did not want to lose him. So I sat in the ambulance and prayed, with my eyes closed tight. My mother thought I was crying and hugged me to her. That was when she began blaming herself.

'Maybe it was the bath,' she said. 'Maybe I shouldn't have made him have a bath. Maybe we should have warmed him up more slowly.' And later: 'He was soaked to the skin, he was shivering. And I just left him sitting there, all that time, in those wet things.'

'It wasn't you,' said my father. 'It was me. I shouldn't have told him about Mum, not straight out like that. I didn't think.'

We sat in casualty at St Margaret's until the early hours of the morning. When I'd come before with my ankle it had been busy, full of interesting injuries. This time there was hardly anyone there to distract me. I tried not to think of Popsicle. I kept picturing him lying there under a white sheet not breathing, not moving. I flicked through all the *Hello!* magazines, all the *National Geographics* and the *Readers Digests* I could find, but I was quite unable to concentrate on any of them. My mother and father both sat grey-faced, like stony statues, and didn't speak to each other, nor to me.

We hadn't had supper and I was hungry. I begged some change off my mother and fed the vending machine. There wasn't much to choose from. I had a meal of Coca Cola, chocolate biscuits and two packets of cheese and onion crisps. I was feeling a bit queasy by the time the doctor finally came to see us.

She was a lot younger than I thought doctors could ever be. She wore jeans and a T-shirt under her white coat, and twiddled her dangling stethoscope around her fingers as if it was a necklace. She smiled an encouraging smile at me, and I knew then that the news was going to be good news. Popsicle was not going to die after all. I wasn't going to lose him. I felt like whooping with joy, but I couldn't, not in a hospital.

'How is he?' my mother asked.

'Stable. We think he's had a stroke, a mild stroke. We'd like to keep him in for a while under observation. We'll do some tests. All being well, he can go back home in a couple of weeks or so. He'll need a bit of looking after. He lives with you, does he?'

'Not really,' said my father. 'Not exactly.'

My mother looked at him meaningfully.

'Well,' my father went on, 'perhaps he does. For the moment anyway.'

The doctor was looking from one to the other in some bewilderment. 'I'm afraid he does seem to have lost some movement in his right side. But given time that should right itself. For a man of his age I'd say he has a very strong constitution. He's very fit. But there is one other thing. He's got a very nasty head wound – fractured his skull in two places. We won't know the extent of the damage – if any – for a while yet. Another reason for keeping a good eye on him.'

'Can we see him?' I asked.

Her bleeper went off. 'No peace for the wicked,' she said. 'The nurse will show you the way.' I watched her walk off down the corridor and decided that if I didn't end up as a concert violinist, or a round-the-world singlehanded yachtswoman, then I'd be a doctor like her – maybe.

Popsicle was lying in a bed surrounded by a fearsome array of monitors and drips. There was a tube in his nose and another in his arm. His hair was gold against the white of the pillows. There was a wide strip of plaster across his forehead, and a dark grey bruise round his eye. He wasn't a pretty sight, but at least the dreadful pallor had gone. He was asleep and breathing deeply, regularly, his mouth wide open. He must have sensed we were there. His eyes opened. For some moments he looked from one to the other of us. He didn't seem to know who we were.

'Not angryla,' he murmured, looking around him. He was more than bewildered, he was frightened, and agitated too. 'Not angryla.' He wasn't making much sense.

'It's me,' I said. 'Cessie. It's all right. You had an accident. You're in hospital. It's all right.' At that he seemed to calm down, and a sudden smile came over his face.

He knew us. He knew me. He beckoned me closer. I bent over him. I was so close I could feel his breath on my cheek. 'See what happens if you eat too many chocolate digestives.'

'It was the sloe gin,' I said, and he managed a smile.

My mother was beside me and taking his hand. 'You've had a bit of a turn,' she said. She was speaking slowly, deliberately and loudly too, as if he were deaf. 'The doctor says you'll be right as rain. We'll come and see you tomorrow, shall we?' Popsicle lifted his hand and touched his forehead. 'You clunked your head, when you fell. You'll have a bit of a shiner too, a black eye. You'll be all right, Popsicle, you'll be fine.'

Popsicle was looking up at my father, trying to lift his head, trying to say something to him. 'Popsicle. You remember, Arthur? It's what you used to call me when you were little. D'you remember?'

'Yes,' said my father.

'And you had big ears in those days too,'

'Did I?'

'And you still have,' Popsicle chuckled just once, and then drifted off to sleep. My father stood there looking down at him. He reached down, took Popsicle's hand and laid it tenderly on the sheet. His hands so wrinkled, so ancient.

'Let's go home,' he said, and he turned on his heel and walked out of the ward without another word.

By the time we got home there wasn't much of the night left, but I spent what there was quite unable to sleep. I kept going over and over in my mind everything that had happened that day. I knew as I lay there in bed that my ordinary life was over, that from now on everything was going to be extraordinary. Popsicle had come out of nowhere, out of the blue, to be my grandfather; and nothing and no one would or could ever be the same again.

4 THE PRODIGAL FATHER

EVERYTHING HAPPENED VERY FAST AFTER THAT.
They didn't want to keep Popsicle in hospital for long,
so we had a lot to do and very little time to do it. The
spare room needed a good lick of paint, and some new
curtains. We set up a radio by his bed, fixed up a
television for him on top of the chest of drawers, and
brought one of the armchairs up from the sitting-
room so he could sit by the window and look out over
the garden.

My father took very little part in all this flurry of
activity, indeed he was scarcely ever home. He did, at
my mother's suggestion, add legs to a wooden tray so
that Popsicle could eat his meals in bed if need be. And
my father took his time over that, disappearing for long
hours into the garden shed where he did his carpentry

– joinery he called it. But whenever he emerged he seemed distant, uneasy somehow. And if ever I asked him about Popsicle – which I often did, and so did my mother – he'd simply shrug and say that it was all a long time ago. Then came the argument over the patchwork quilt.

It was the morning we were due to bring Popsicle home from the hospital. My mother and I were upstairs in what was to be Popsicle's room and I was helping her to spread out the old family patchwork quilt. It fitted the bed perfectly.

'1925,' she said, showing me the date sewn into one of the corners. 'The year Popsicle was born, if I've worked it out right. Looks fine, doesn't it, Cessie?'

She stood back and looked around the room. 'I want it all to be special for him, Cessie, really special.'

At that moment my father came in and at once noticed the quilt. 'Don't you think you're overdoing it a bit?' he said. 'You always said that quilt was too good to use. Unique, you said. Part of your family history. He'll get food on it. Bound to. It'll spoil.'

'What is the matter with you, Arthur?' my mother said. 'It's for your father, isn't it? To make him feel at home. Don't you want him to feel at home?' She didn't wait for him to reply. 'Well, I do. This is *my* family heirloom, made by *my* great aunt, and I want him to have it on his bed.' She touched his arm as she passed him to open the window. 'Come on, Arthur. I just want him to feel welcome, that's all – you know, like the fatted calf and the prodigal son.'

'With one big difference,' my father said. 'This isn't the prodigal son come back home, it's the prodigal father. And we hardly know him. You don't know him. I don't know him. I just think you're laying it on too much, that's all.' My mother was looking at him long and hard. I knew that look, and my father did too. He turned away.

'I may not be back till late,' he said, and he was gone.

'Won't you even be here when we bring him back?' she called after him. He didn't reply.

My father wasn't there when we came home with Popsicle that evening. Popsicle never asked where he was, so we didn't need to excuse or explain or lie. 'He'll be busy at work, I expect,' was all he said. But he caught my eye, and I could see how hurt he was, how disappointed.

Popsicle spent those first ten days or so of his convalescence up in the bedroom that had become his. He slept a lot, either propped up on his pillows in bed, or in his armchair by the window. With his head bandaged, he looked less like the Viking warlord I had first known, and more like an Apache warrior. He had his meals up there, and the bathroom was right next door, so he never needed to come downstairs at all.

Whenever my father wasn't about – and he wasn't about these days – the three of us settled into a routine of our own. My mother would cook. I would ferry trays up and down the stairs. I would cut up Popsicle's food and she would help bathe him – his right arm was almost useless, though he could walk unaided by now. I'd play him my violin whenever he wanted me to, and that was often. 'I love a good tune,' he told me. 'Scott Joplin, George Formby, Vera Lynn, Elvis, the Beatles, you name it and I'll sing it. I know them all, off the radio.' I soon discovered he was particularly passionate about the Beatles. He'd hum me through one of their songs. I'd practise it and then play it back for him. 'Yesterday', 'Yellow Submarine', 'Norwegian Wood' – he taught me them all, and then sang along with me, once I'd got the hang of the tunes. Strictly speaking this wasn't violin practice, but I counted it as such – and it was a lot more fun.

Sometimes, though, he was happy just to sit in his chair for hours and watch the goldcrests flitting about the garden or the swallows swooping down to drink from the goldfish pond. Watching alongside him, I learnt more about birds in a few days than I'd learnt in my entire life.

But whether it was birdwatching or the Beatles, when it was time for one of my father's radio shows, everything else was forgotten. We had to promise always to remind him, even to wake him if he was asleep.

The radio had to be turned on well before time, just to be sure he didn't miss the beginning of each show. It was the highlight of his day. He had only to hear my father's voice and his whole face would at once be suffused with loving pride.

I just wished my father would be home more often, for Popsicle's sake, and for mine too. He never came to hear me play my violin these days. He just didn't seem interested any more. My mother said he was overtired, working too hard, but I felt there was more to it than that.

Dr Wickens used to come in every few days to check on Popsicle, and a nurse would call daily to change the dressing on his head. There would be hushed and confidential discussions as my mother, or my father, or both, walked them out of the front door and up the path, always out of earshot. From their faces and from everyone's reluctance to answer my questions, I knew something was not quite right, but I had no idea what it was. I wasn't that worried either, because Popsicle was getting out and about now much more. There was already more use in his arm, that was obvious, and he was up and down the stairs like a yo-yo.

Dr Wickens had recommended gentle exercise; but said he mustn't get cold. So, every day now, with Popsicle well wrapped up in his coat, and in what he called my 'Rupert Bear' scarf, we would walk slowly down the road to the park. It wasn't far. My mother made him carry a stick, on the principle that three legs are safer, more reliable, than two. Popsicle didn't like it but he went along with it.

To begin with, I dreaded going on these walks. I was forever worried about bumping into Shirley and Mandy, my tormentors from school; but once we'd discovered the ducks, I forgot all about them. Popsicle adored ducks. To sweeten them in close he'd make wonderful ducky noises, quite indistinguishable from the real thing. We'd sit there on the bench, and wait till we were completely surrounded, and deafened by a chorus of raucous quacking. When he was quite sure they were all there, he'd dig deep into his bag of crusts and hurl them as far as he could out on to the pond. How he'd chuckle to watch them go, and how he hated to leave them when the time came. 'Back tomorrow,' he'd tell them. And we always were.

He loved the garden too. When it was warm we'd often find him out there, picking weeds off the rockery or raking the lawn. He liked to be up and doing, he said.

But I did notice that he was a little wrapped up in himself these days, as if he were lost in his thoughts and didn't know the way out. I'd often find him sitting in his armchair just staring ahead into space. Sometimes he wouldn't even know I was there till I spoke to him.

If he was brooding, I thought, then perhaps he had good reason. My father hardly ever seemed to speak to him, not unless he had to. Whenever they were in the same room together, it was always uncomfortable. All too often, my father would find it suddenly very important to be elsewhere. As he left the room, the hurt on Popsicle's face was plain to see.

It wasn't until some time later that I was to discover what all this was about. My father was home late again after work. They must have thought I was already asleep, but I wasn't. Popsicle had turned off his radio in his room so I could hear quite plainly every word they were saying downstairs in the kitchen.

'But have you asked him again?' My father's voice.

'I can't keep asking him, Arthur. It upsets him. And,

anyway, asking him isn't going to help. It isn't going to make it come back, is it? You just have to accept it. You know what Dr Wickens said. It wasn't the stroke that's caused it. He told us. He explained it all. The brain's nothing more than a jelly, a blancmange, and the skull's there to protect it. You jolt the skull violently enough, you bash the brain up against the inside of the skull, and it can cause serious damage, bruising, bleeding, whatever. The result can be some loss of memory, temporary or otherwise. So it's hardly surprising that Popsicle can't seem to remember much, is it? If he says he can't remember where he lives, where he's from or anything else, then I believe him. And I simply can't understand why you don't.'

'All right, then tell me this, how come he still remembers Bradwell? Answer me that. He goes on and on about the old days when I was a kid in Bradwell. As far as I can see he remembers anyone and everyone from those days. And that was forty, fifty years ago. Yet he can't seem to remember where he lived before he walked in here four weeks ago. Now doesn't that strike you as a little strange?'

'Not really. My memory's fairly patchy already, and I'm only thirty-six years old, and I haven't just fractured my skull in two places. But you don't mean "strange" do you, Arthur? You mean convenient. Why don't you come right out with it. You just don't want him here, do you?'

'What do you expect? He's a complete stranger to me. I don't know the man.' He was almost shouting now. I could hear my mother shushing him to lower his voice. 'Listen,' he went on, just as loudly. 'Let's say you're right, let's say he *has* lost his memory – which I doubt – who says it'll ever come back again? Who says he'll ever remember where he comes from? He can't go on living here for ever, can he?'

'I don't know why not. He's not much trouble. And, besides, you're never here these days, are you? What's it matter to you?' He seemed temporarily silenced by that. My mother hadn't finished with him yet. 'For God's sake, Arthur. He's an old man. He's got no one else, so far as we can tell, and nowhere else to go. After all those years he's found his son and you've found your father. Doesn't that mean anything to you?'

My father was speaking much more calmly now, so that I had to get out of bed and put my ear to the floor-boards to be able to hear him at all. 'Of course it means something,' he was saying, 'but I'm not sure what, that's all.' He didn't go on for some moments. 'Listen, there's things you don't know, things I haven't told you.'

'What things?'

'It's what my mother told me about him. She said he'd get mad in the head sometimes. "Mad with sadness", she called it. One moment high as a kite, the next down in the dumps. And he was a bit of a layabout, couldn't hold down a job, always in trouble, drank too much, that sort of thing. My mother didn't want to leave him. She had to. That's what she told me, and I believe her. I didn't ask him to come here, did I? He just landed on us, and now he comes up with this fantastical tale that he can't remember where he's from, nor where he lives. And you believe him, just like that! Well, I'm afraid I don't. And now maybe you understand why I don't. I've had enough. I'm going to bed.'

I heard the kitchen door open and my father's footsteps on the stairs. I was tempted to jump out of bed and confront him there and then, and tell him just what I thought of him. But I didn't dare. I heard my mother crying down below in the kitchen. Whenever she cried, I cried. I couldn't help myself. I cried into my pillow, not only in sympathy but in anger too. I hated my father that night for making her cry and I hated him too for saying what he had about Popsicle. I hardly slept at all. I lay there full of doubts and forebodings.

By morning I had determined to find out how much

of what I'd overheard was true. I would talk to Popsicle and find out for myself exactly how much he could remember, and how much he couldn't. I would try to do it in such a way that I wouldn't upset him. I would try to be casual.

The next morning we were both in Popsicle's room. I was tightening my violin bow. 'But before you came here, Popsicle,' I began as nonchalantly as I could, 'where did you live?'

'Ah,' he said. 'You too.' And I wished at once I hadn't asked. 'So they told you. I asked them not to. Didn't want you worrying.' He sighed. 'How I wish I knew, Cessie, but I don't. And that's the honest truth of it. I don't remember. I remember ringing the bell on your front door. I can remember you coming down the stairs, and I can remember Patsy too in the bath. But that's all. I remember bits and pieces from long ago: Bradwell, and Cecilia, and little Arthur – all that. We had some good times, Cessie, good times, believe me. And songs. Don't know why, but I seem to remember songs. "Yellow Submarine", "Nowhere Man", lots of them. Clear as a bell, I remember them. And my poems too, I haven't lost them, thank God. Keep me sane, they do. But as for the rest, Cessie, it's gone, all gone. It's like living in a fog. I'm not lying to you, Cessie. Honestly.'

I thought of asking more, of probing more deeply, but I couldn't. I knew enough anyway, enough to know that I believed him, believed him absolutely.

I waited until my father came home that evening, late again. Popsicle had gone up to bed. I'd been waiting all day for just the moment and now the moment was right. I went storming into the sitting-room.

'It's not fair.' I was in tears already. 'It's not fair. I heard you. Last night, I heard you. Popsicle can't help it. He fell and hit his head. He had a stroke. That's not his fault, is it?' I had the advantage of surprise. They were both gaping at me. 'He'd never have had a stroke in the first place if you hadn't . . .'

'Cessie!' My mother was trying to stop me, but I was steaming with fury. Nothing would stop me now.

'He's not making it up, Dad. I know he isn't. But even if he was, I wouldn't mind. I like having him here and I want him to stay. I want him to stay forever if he wants to. I hate all this . . . feeling in the air. Do you know what I wish? I wish . . . I wish you weren't my father.' I ran out and upstairs to my room where I slammed my door as hard as I could.

They left me for a few minutes, and then my father came up to my room and sat on my bed. I kept my back to him.

'It's not easy for you to understand what's going on here, Cessie,' he began. 'Not easy for me either. I never had a real father, you see, not till now. I had a stepfather for a while, of course, but it's not the same; and anyway, Bill and me, we never got on. I don't know what you do with a father, how you talk to a father. You've got to trust me. I'll do right by him, I promise you that. But you don't love a father just because he's your father. You can't love someone you don't know, and I don't know him. You've got to give me time, Cessie.'

I was still seething, still too angry to turn over. I wanted to, but I couldn't bring myself to do it. I'd said things I shouldn't have said, and I knew it. He leant over and kissed the back of my head. 'I'm not an ogre, Cessie,' he whispered. 'Honestly.' When he said 'honestly', he sounded just like Popsicle.

The next morning I was up late. There was no sound of the radio from Popsicle's room, so I thought he must be downstairs, having his breakfast already. But I found my mother alone in the kitchen. She was pouring herself a cup of coffee as I came in. 'Well,' she said, 'that was some performance last night.'

'Sorry,' I said.

'No, you're not.' She was not angry with me, but she was not pleased either. 'Popsicle up yet?' she went on.

'He can do almost everything for himself now, you know, except for cutting his food up. Marvellous how that arm of his has come on. Let's just hope his memory does the same. Go and see if he's all right, Cessie, will you?'

The bathroom door was ajar. He was not in there. There was no reply when I knocked on his bedroom door. I went in. His bed was made. The wardrobe door was open. His clothes were gone, his coat too, and there were no shoes by the bed. He'd gone. Popsicle had gone.

5 NOWHERE MAN

MY MOTHER SAT DOWN ON THE BED, THE POINTS of her fingers pressed against her temples, her eyes closed for a moment in concentration. 'Think,' she said. 'We've got to think.'

It came to me at once. 'Ducks,' I said. 'Maybe he's feeding the ducks.' We dashed downstairs. We found what we'd hoped to find, that the bag of accumulated bread-crusts we kept for the ducks was no longer hanging on the back of the kitchen door. A further search revealed that his stick was gone too.

'I'll take the car,' said my mother. 'You stay here, in case he comes home. He'll be in the park, bound to be. Shan't be long. And don't worry.'

She *was* long and I *was* worried. It seemed like an age before she came back, but when she did she was alone.

I met her at the front door. She had Popsicle's stick in her hand. 'He's been there, but he's not there any more. I've looked everywhere. He left it on the bench. And this too.' She held out the breadcrust bag. It was empty. 'I asked around. No one's seen him. It's like he's just disappeared.'

'He can't have,' I cried. 'You can't just disappear. No one can.'

She reached out and smoothed my hair tenderly. 'You're right, Cessie. We'll find him, I promise we will. I've tried ringing your dad at work, but he's off somewhere, doing an interview or something. I tried his mobile too. Nothing. Only one thing to do. I'm going down to the police station. You'd better stay here. He'll probably walk in just as soon as I've gone. Worrying won't help, Cessie. Go and practise your violin or something – it'll keep your mind off it.' And she was gone.

I tried practising. I tried reading. I tried the television. Nothing worked. It was impossible not to think of all the dreadful things that might have happened to Popsicle. He'd had another stroke. He'd been run over. He'd fallen into the canal. Or maybe he'd just gone off as suddenly as he'd arrived, and would never be coming back again.

As the minutes passed by like hours, I was more and more certain that this was in fact what had happened. Perhaps he'd suddenly remembered where he lived and had just gone home. Miserable though this made me, I consoled myself with the thought that at least he wasn't hurt, at least he wasn't dead.

My mother did come back eventually, and when she did she was beside herself with indignation. 'If it was a child, they'd be out there looking for him right now – dogs, helicopters, the lot. "How long has he been gone?" he says. "Maybe he's just wandered off, madam. They do, y'know. We can't go looking for every OAP who decides to take a longer walk than usual, can we now, madam?" God, did I give him an earful! So finally he says, "All right, madam, all right. We'll give it an hour or two and if he's still not back then we'll go looking, how's that? Meanwhile, I'll ask the lads to keep an eye out, madam." I'll give him madam! Well if they won't look, I will. I'm going to drive around town till I find him. He can't have gone far. I want you to stay here, Cessie, and I want you to try your dad, and keep trying. Understand?' And despite all my protestations, she went running off up the path, leaving me alone in the house again.

I rang my father every few minutes, both at work

and on his mobile. When at long last he answered, it took me a bit by surprise. 'Popsicle's gone,' I said. 'He's gone, and we can't find him.' He didn't say anything, so I told him the rest. Even after I'd finished the whole story, he still said nothing.

'Dad?' I said. 'You there?'

'I'm here.'

'Mum's gone off looking for him,' I repeated. 'And the police won't do anything.'

I have no idea what he said, nor to whom he said it, but within five minutes there was a police car outside the house and two policemen at the front door. 'So you've lost your grandaddy, have you?' said the taller of the two, taking off his cap. The other one had a mermaid tattooed on his arm. 'Your mum and dad in, are they?' said the tattooed one. And they walked right past me into the house as if they owned the place. They never asked. They just wandered about the house, peering into this room and that. They even went out into the garden and searched the garden shed. Did they really imagine they'd find Popsicle hiding away in the garden shed?

My father came home, and then my mother shortly after. There followed a prolonged question-and-answer session around the kitchen table over endless cups of tea, all about Popsicle, where he went, what he did.

'Have you got any photos of him?'

'No.'

'Not one?'

'No. Well, there is one of him as a young man. But it's in his wallet and he must have his wallet with him.'

'Do you know who his friends are?'

'I'm afraid not.'

'How long has he been living with you?'

'A month or so.'

'And before that?'

'We don't know,' said my father.

The more we didn't know, the more strange they seemed to find it all. A third policeman came in, filling the doorway. They had already checked all the hospitals for miles around, he said, and no one of Popsicle's description had been brought in. No one had seen him. It was just as my mother had said, Popsicle had disappeared.

She seemed suddenly very dejected. The tattooed policeman leant forward across the table. 'Listen,' he said. 'It's true what they say: no news *is* good news. You just sit right here, and we'll keep on looking till we find him.' He gave me a cheery wink as he stood up again.

But by six o'clock that evening, after the longest day

of my life, there was still no news of Popsicle, good or bad. 'I need a walk,' said my mother. 'I've got to get out. I can't stand any more of this waiting.'

'Nor me,' I said.

This time my father stayed by the phone. As we left, he said, 'He'll turn up, you'll see. That old man's a survivor. He'll turn up.' He never called him 'my father' or 'Popsicle', and I wished he would.

We ended up in the park – I'm not sure why. There was a large crowd gathered round the duck pond, so we couldn't even see the bench where we usually sat with Popsicle, nor the pond beyond. We had to force our way through the crowd to see what was going on. There were a couple of policemen holding everyone back, not the same ones who had come to the house. I heard a sudden agitated quacking commotion from the middle of the pond, and a flurry of ducks took off and circled over the park. My mother grasped me by the arm. I looked where she was looking. Out of the pond rose first one head, then two. Frogmen. Frogmen in goggles and wetsuits, with oxygen tanks on their backs. My mother had her hand to her mouth. She knew what I knew, that they were dragging the pond for Popsicle.

I led her home in tears, and the three of us sat in the kitchen in silence, just waiting, fearing the worst, believing the worst. There were more encouraging words of reassurance from my father, but we didn't believe them, and I don't think he did either. I tried to pray as I had in the ambulance. After all, it had worked that time, hadn't it? But I couldn't concentrate long enough even to finish a prayer. I had a picture floating in my head that would not go away, a picture of Popsicle, drowned, lying face down in the pond, his hair spread out over the water like golden seaweed.

Then came the knock on the door. Both my mother and father seemed paralysed, so I had to go and open it myself. It was the police again. This time one of them was a woman, and behind her was the one with the tattoo on his arm.

'May we come in?' she said. Dark and dreadful words that fell like stones on my heart. Tears choked my throat. They'd found Popsicle, I knew it. They'd found him dead and drowned and I'd never even said goodbye. I took them into the kitchen. 'We've found him,' said the policewoman. 'Down by the harbour. He was just sitting there looking at the boats. Just sitting there. He's fine, fine.'

My mother was sobbing. I found myself sobbing too and I couldn't stop myself. My father had his arms round both of us. 'Didn't I tell you?' he said. 'Didn't I tell you?'

'He's a very confused old man,' the policewoman went on. 'Didn't seem to know where he was nor how he'd got himself there. We took him off to the hospital. Routine check-up. Can't be too careful, can you? Not when they get to that age.'

'They'll be bringing him home soon,' said the tattooed policeman. 'All being well, he should be back in time for supper. Bit scatty in the head, I'd say. Bit forgetful like, is he?'

The ambulance brought Popsicle home from the hospital that same evening. I was overjoyed to see that the neighbours were out in numbers yet again. As we fetched him into the house, I waved regally at Mandy Bethel. I enjoyed that.

All through supper no one said a word about Popsicle's disappearance – that had been my mother's idea. 'He'll tell us when he wants to,' she'd said. Popsicle carried on as if nothing had happened. He sat there, quite at home, waiting for me to cut up his pork chop for him. Then he ate ravenously, chuckling to himself as he chased his peas around his plate with his fork until he'd speared the very last one.

'Gotcha,' he laughed, popping it in his mouth with a flourish. He pushed his plate away and sat back. There came the moment then when we were all looking at him, and waiting, and he knew well enough what we were waiting for.

'Was I hungry!' he said. 'I haven't eaten since breakfast, you know.'

'You could have come home sooner,' said my father, and I could sense him reining in his exasperation, with some difficulty. 'For goodness' sake, you were gone all day.'

Popsicle was looking straight at my father as he spoke. 'What Cessie said last night, I heard every word. I didn't want to cause any more upsets, that's all. Time to pack up and go, I thought. So I did. I got up early and I just went. I was sitting there down in the park, feeding the ducks, and I was wondering what to do with myself, where to go. That's when it came to me. This is just like where I live, I thought, by the water, with ducks and gulls and all sorts. So I went off looking, looking for my place. I thought the best bet would be down by the harbour, along the seafront. I thought I'd maybe see something, something I'd recognise. Where I live, I can see water out of every window. I can smell the sea too, I know I can. So I went looking. Walked miles, I did. I looked at every house along the sea front, in the windows of some of them. Got myself shouted at too. But it wasn't any good. I didn't recognise a thing.'

'I still don't understand,' my father said. 'All right, so you upped and went, went off looking for your house. But when you couldn't find it, why didn't you just come back here? We've been worried sick, all of us.'

'I couldn't,' said Popsicle. 'I didn't know where I was, where I'd come from, or anything. I couldn't even remember the name of this street, so I couldn't ask, could I? I mean, you don't want to look stupid, do you? So I just sat myself down and tried to piece it all together, you know, work it out, make some sense of it. I could see you all up here in my head. I could see this house, this kitchen, my room upstairs, the garden, everything; but I didn't know where you all were, nor how to get to you. That's my trouble. Sometimes things are as clear as day, and sometimes . . . well, ever since I was in the hospital . . . You take your mum for instance, Arthur. I can't picture her like I used to. I know what she looked like from her photo; but I can't see her up here.' He tapped his head with his knuckles. 'When I think of your mum now, it's not her face that comes into my head, I know it's not. It's someone else, always someone else altogether, but I don't know who.' For a few moments, he seemed quite unable to find his voice. He looked at us, his eyes brimming with sadness. He was trying to smile, but he couldn't. 'A nowhere man, that's me. A real nowhere man, like the song says.'

'Things'll come back, Popsicle,' said my mother. 'Time's a great healer. Things'll sort themselves out.' She reached out and took his hand in hers. 'You're family now,' she said. 'You're family, and you're staying. You belong here with us. We want you to stay as long as you like. Isn't that right, Arthur?'

We had to wait some moments for my father to reply, and when he did it was not at all fulsome. 'Of course,' he said. 'Of course we do.' That was all. I was angry at him again, angry at his thinly disguised reluctance. Maybe he had his reasons, but he could pretend a little, couldn't he? Just to make Popsicle feel at home and welcome. He could pretend.

'But you've got to promise you won't go off on your wanders again,' said my mother, wagging her finger playfully at Popsicle. 'Frightened us half to death, you did. Promise?'

'Promise,' Popsicle replied, holding up his hand. 'Cross my heart and hope to die.'

'We don't want you doing that either,' she said, and we all laughed at that, even my father.

'Well,' my mother went on, getting to her feet, 'now that's settled, we can get on with life, can't we? And you know what that means, don't you, Cessie Stevens?'

'No.' But I knew exactly what she was getting at.

'I have this feeling that, in all the excitement, you might have forgotten something.' I played dumb. 'Your violin practice?' There was no point in arguing. I made the best of it and got up to leave.

'You want me to come up and hear you?' my father asked.

'It's all right,' I replied. I was so angry with him, and I wanted him to know it. 'Popsicle'll come, won't you? We'll do some Beatles songs.'

' "Nowhere Man",' said Popsicle, as I helped him to his feet. 'We'll do "Nowhere Man".'

So we went upstairs and, sitting on the bed in my room, Popsicle taught me 'Nowhere Man' till I knew it through and through. I played. He sang. We were good together, very good. But my mind wasn't on it. I just couldn't enjoy it as much as I usually did. I kept thinking of my father downstairs, and I kept wishing I hadn't been so cruel.

When I'd finished, Popsicle looked at me for a while, and then he said, 'You and me, we're friends, aren't we? And friends have to be honest with each other, right?'

'Yes.'

'You've always been good to me, Cessie. You spoke up for me last night, and I shan't forget that, not ever.

But you mustn't judge your dad like you do. You mustn't hurt him. You're the apple of his eye, you are. So you be kind to him, eh? There's a girl.'

Popsicle had been reading my mind again, and I wondered how he did it.

6 AND ALL SHALL BE WELL

IT WAS SOON AFTER THIS THAT I BEGAN TO NOTICE Popsicle talking to himself. I'd hear him in his bedroom, a muffled monologue, so muffled that I could never make out much of what he was saying. I noticed too that he was becoming more and more absent-minded. Once, he went wandering out into the garden in the rain with just his socks on; and time and again he'd make the tea and forget to put any tea in the pot. He'd think that lunch-time was tea-time and tea-time was lunch-time. Every time he'd try to laugh it off and call himself a 'silly old codger', but I could see that it worried him as much as it worried us.

Then one day he lit a bonfire too close to the garden shed and Mr Goldsmith's fence. I wasn't at home when it happened. I was out at Madame Poitou's for my violin lesson. When I came back the fire-engine was already there and a pall of brown smoke was hanging over the house. I ran inside. Popsicle was sitting on the bottom stair in the hallway, his face in his hands, and my mother was crouched down beside him trying to comfort him.

'It's not your fault, Popsicle,' she was saying. 'These things happen. Why don't you go upstairs and have a nice wash? You'll feel a lot better.' His eyes were red, his face tear-stained and besmirched. He went up the stairs very slowly.

I followed my mother out into the garden. It was a mess out there, a real mess. The fire-fighters were packing up and going. As one of them passed us, he stopped. 'Could have been a lot worse, missus. Whatever does he think he was doing anyway? First he builds a bonfire too close to the shed and then he goes off and leaves it. Got to be a bit doolally, if you ask me.'

When they had all gone I gave her a hand tidying up what we could in the garden. We raked all that was left of the garden shed into a pile of charred timbers and soggy ashes. She worried on and on about what Mr Goldsmith from next door would say about his fence when he got home from work. And she worried on about Popsicle too.

We were an hour or so clearing up the worst of it. My wellingtons were covered in mud by this time, so I had to take them off at the back door before I went in. I was padding through the hallway into the kitchen when I felt it. The carpet was sodden under my bare feet. I charged upstairs to find the basin overflowing, and the bathroom awash. I turned off the tap and pulled out the plug.

Popsicle was in his room, sitting on his bed and staring into space. I sat down beside him.

'It doesn't matter, Popsicle,' I said. 'It's just a rotten old garden shed. It was falling down anyway. Dad's been moaning on about it ever since we moved here. He was going to get a new one. Honestly he was.' But nothing I could say seemed to bring him any comfort.

Then he muttered something, something I couldn't quite hear. 'Sorry?' I said, leaning closer.

'Shangri-La.' He clutched at my hand as he spoke. 'Shangri-La, I don't want to go to Shangri-La.' I could see in his eyes that he was terrified. He was pleading with me, begging me.

'What's Shangri-La?' There was an echo in my head, an echo of something he'd said before.

'I don't know. I don't know.' The tears were running down his cheeks, and he didn't even trouble to wipe them away.

'If you don't want to go there,' I said, 'then no one's going to make you, I promise.' He seemed happier at that.

'You promise?' he said. I laid my head on his shoulder, and after a while I felt his arm come round me. That was how my mother found us some time later. She helped Popsicle to wash, and put him to bed.

We spent the rest of the day mopping up. But there was still water dripping from the lightbulb into a bucket in the hallway when my father came in from work. I explained what had happened, how none of it had been Popsicle's fault, just bad luck, that's all. 'Anyway,' I said, 'now you can have your new garden shed like you wanted.'

They exchanged knowing glances. I knew then that they were both, in some way, blaming Popsicle for what had happened. My father walked out into the garden to inspect the damage and left the two of us alone. It was then I remembered what Popsicle had said to me earlier.

'Where's Shangri-La?' I asked my mother.

'Why?' she said.

'I just wondered. Read it in a book somewhere.' I didn't want to say any more.

'Well,' she said, 'it's a sort of imaginary paradise, high up in the mountains, the Himalayas, I think. A kind of heaven on earth, you could call it. Just a story of course. Doesn't exist, not really.'

But I couldn't forget the fear in Popsicle's eyes when he'd spoken of it. Imaginary or not, Shangri-La was real enough to him.

After the garden-shed fire, I would often find myself alone in the house with Popsicle. My mother was in and out of school getting ready for the new school year; and my father, of course, was as busy as ever down at the radio station, always leaving the house early and getting home late. I was to keep a watchful eye on Popsicle; and above all, they said, I mustn't let him wander off on his own. As it turned out, he didn't seem to want to. He seemed to be as content with my company as I was with his. Having Popsicle at home was a boon for me. I was dreading going back to school, because I knew I'd have to face Shirley Watson and the others. Just the thought of them looking at me, laughing at me, made me go cold inside, but Popsicle kept my mind off all that – most of the time anyway.

We did everything together. He'd listen to me playing my violin, and I'd listen to him reciting his favourite poems. It was strange. He couldn't even remember where he lived, but he knew his poems off by heart, dozens of them. I wasn't sure I always understood them, but I loved listening to him, because when Popsicle read poetry he made the words sing.

What he still looked forward to most though was our daily walk to the park to feed the ducks. Once out there in the park he just loved to talk, never about his past though, and never about my father. He loved to think out loud. As with the poems, I have to say I couldn't always follow all of it, but I listened all the same because I knew he was confiding in me, trusting in me, and I felt honoured by that.

The day it happened we were on our way back home from the park. We had to stop at the shop for some milk. He was tired by this time, but that never stopped him talking. 'Have you ever thought, Cessie?' he was saying. 'Have you ever thought that this is all a dream? All of it, the ducks, the pond, this shop, you, me, all of it, nothing but a funny old dream. Maybe all you do when you die is wake up, and then you don't remember anything anyway because you never remember dreams, do you? You know what they say, Cessie? They say in the last two minutes before you die you live your whole life over again. Looks like I'll have to wait till then to remember. Be a bit late by then, bit late to do anything about it, I mean.' He was frowning now. There's something I've still got to put right, Cessie, I know there is, something I've got to do. Trouble is, I can't for the life of me remember what it is.'

We were inside the shop by now and walking along past the breakfast cereals and the coffee and the tea, towards the fridge at the back. Popsicle had stopped talking. I was a while finding the two-litre carton of semi-skimmed I was looking for. When I turned round Popsicle had vanished. I panicked, but I needn't have. I found him almost at once near the check-out desk. He had taken a tin off the shelf.

'What've you got?' I asked him.

'There's something, Cessie, something I've remembered,' he said.

I read the label out loud. 'Condensed milk?'

'All I know is that I like it,' he went on, 'that I've always liked it.' He was looking at me strangely, as if I wasn't there. 'There were searchlights. There were searchlights and I couldn't get out. I couldn't get out.'

'What d'you mean?' I asked.

'I don't know, Cessie. That's the trouble, I don't know what I mean. But this, this tin is part of what I've got to remember, I know it is. I can't think, Cessie, I can't think.' His eyes were tight closed and he was banging the tin repeatedly against the side of his head. Everyone was looking at us now, so I bought the milk and the tin of condensed milk, took Popsicle by the arm and left the shop as quickly as I could. All the way home he was lost in himself, and that was how he stayed.

After that he wouldn't go out for his walk any more. He wouldn't read his poetry. He'd simply sit in his chair in the sitting-room, frowning incessantly and gazing into nowhere. If ever I offered to play my violin for him, he'd just shake his head. Whatever my mother put on his plate he refused to touch, not even pancakes and maple syrup, and he adored pancakes and maple syrup. 'The look of it doesn't taste nice,' he said. He said such odd things these days. She was worried about him, and I could see my father was too; but I wasn't. I knew what they didn't know, that he'd discovered a clue to his past and was struggling to work out what it meant. Once he'd worked it out, then the door to his memory would open and everything would be fine. I was sure of it.

Each night I lay awake wondering what the significance of a tin of condensed milk could possibly be. I asked myself again and again whether or not I should tell anyone about it, but I decided that what passed between Popsicle and me when we were alone was our private business and no one else's. I felt it would be like informing on him, like breaking a confidence. So I said nothing.

Popsicle had hardly eaten a thing now for a week. He was so frail he had to be helped up the stairs to bed. He didn't shave any more. He didn't wash any more. He never got out of his dressing-gown and slippers. Nothing seemed to interest him. He'd even stopped listening to my father on the radio. All day and every day, he'd just sit there rocking back and forth, humming tunes to himself and rubbing his knees. Like Aladdin, I thought, like Aladdin rubbing his lamp. He was making a wish and rubbing, but, unlike Aladdin, no amount of rubbing brought out the genie to make his wish come true. I was watching him sink deeper and deeper into despair and there was nothing I could do about it.

My mother tried all she knew. She tried threats. 'You don't eat this and I won't ever make you pancakes again.' She tried blackmail. 'You don't go out and feed those ducks of yours and they'll die.'

My father tried sweet-talking Popsicle out of it, but he very soon gave up in exasperation.

'If you ask me,' he said, 'he's just being downright difficult. My mother always said he was a moody devil. She wasn't far wrong either.'

'How can you say that?' I cried. 'He's not doing it deliberately. He's just sad, that's all. He's trying to remember, and he can't. How would you like it, if you'd lost your memory?' Tears of anger always came too easily to me, and I wished they wouldn't. He was judging Popsicle, blaming him, and that was so unjust, and so unfair.

Then one evening they called in Dr Wickens. He spent a good half hour alone with Popsicle. I sat on the stairs outside and tried to eavesdrop – unsuccessfully – until my mother found me and fetched me into the kitchen, where all three of us sat and waited.

It was some time before the doctor came into the kitchen. He sat down heavily, and packed his stethoscope into his black bag. He smiled at me over his glasses.

'Well,' he began, 'I've had a good look at him. The good news is that he's continuing to make a good recovery from the stroke. His right arm's not as strong as I'd like it to be just yet, but apart from that he's got the constitution of an ox. He's got a thumping strong heart, and his blood pressure's fine. Lungs as clear as a bell.' He paused.

'So what's the bad news?' my father asked.

'Well, I don't think it's that serious, not yet, but he is depressed. He won't talk to me much, so I can't say how depressed exactly. Depression is not uncommon after a stroke. And of course there's this loss of memory. That can't have helped. So he's going to need some treatment.'

'What sort of treatment?' my mother asked.

'Hopefully, it can be dealt with by a short course of antidepressant pills. And perhaps a spell in a nursing home may be necessary for a while. We'll see. Let's hope it won't come to that. The pills should set him right, get him eating again, get him on his feet, help him take more of an interest in life.'

So they did, and when the transformation came, it came so soon and so suddenly that it took us all completely by surprise. It was two or three days later, on Sunday afternoon. My father was out in the garden, rebuilding the fence with Mr Goldsmith, who had been very good about it, considering everything. My mother was ironing in the sitting-room – again. I was curled up with a book on the sofa – a six-pages-a-minute horror book. Popsicle was upstairs lying down on his bed, as he had been more and more often just recently. He'd eaten a little bit of his lunch – we'd all noticed that – but he'd been just as uncommunicative as ever. Suddenly we heard him calling out. 'Up here,' he cried. 'Cessie, come up here!' I was upstairs in an instant, my mother hard on my heels.

He was sitting up in his bed and chuckling. The tin of condensed milk was open on his lap and he was licking the spoon clean. He held up the tin to show us. It was quite empty. 'Cessie,' he said, 'I've got a riddle for you. Do you know why elephants have good memories?'

'No,' I said. 'Why do elephants have good memories?'

'Because they eat a lot,' he said, wagging the spoon at me. '*And* . . .' Now he was wagging it at my mother. '*And* because they wash themselves too.' He rubbed his stubbly chin, and was grinning hugely. '*And* maybe, just maybe, because they shave as well, every day.'

'Popsicle.' My mother put her arms round him and hugged him. 'Popsicle, you're better. You're feeling better, aren't you?'

'A whole heap, and I'm not talking elephants either – if you know what I mean.' And at that his chuckling broke into guffaws of laughter.

'What *is* this stuff?' my mother asked, taking the empty tin off him. She was wrinkling her nose at it disapprovingly.

'Ah,' said Popsicle enigmatically. 'That's magic that is, pure magic.' He swung his legs off the bed. 'Give us a hand up, Cessie, there's a girl.' He was standing between us, still holding on to my arm, when my father came into the room.

The two of them looked at each other, and for a while neither seemed to know what to say.

'Put you all through it a bit, didn't I?' said Popsicle.

'A bit,' my father agreed.

'Black dog days. I've always had them, all my life. I don't rightly know how I get into them. But I'm out now, and all on account of a tin of condensed milk. Got me thinking.' He steadied himself against my shoulder.

'Well, I suppose it's about time this old elephant had a wash and brush-up,' he said, and without another word he went off to the bathroom. It wasn't long before we heard him singing 'Yellow Submarine', full volume too.

To my mother's huge delight and relief, before he went to bed that night he ate three syrupy pancakes, and downed two mugs of hot chocolate, five spoonfuls of sugar in each. That tin of condensed milk had reminded him of something, and something important too, I was sure of it. I waited until he was in bed, and then I went in to see him. He was reading.

'T.S. Eliot,' he said. 'Good poet, he is. Listen to this:

"And all shall be well and
All manner of things shall be well"

He's right too.'

'You know something, don't you?' I said. 'You know where you live. You've remembered, haven't you?'

'No. I'm afraid not, Cessie. But I'm getting there. I've made a start.'

'What then? What've you remembered?'

'It's only a little thing, but a little thing is something. Every night when I'm home, I have three teaspoons of condensed milk, always have done. Helps me sleep. Helps me think straight. I can see them lined up on the shelf above the sink in my kitchen – dozens of tins of condensed milk. I can see them, up here in my head. Only a little kitchen – not enough room to swing a rat, let alone a cat. I'm telling you, Cessie, it's coming. All I need is my condensed milk each night to oil the old memory. It'll get it working again, I know it will.'

'Are you having me on?'

'Cross my heart, Cessie. It works. Honestly. I mean, look at me. I'm feeling better already. That's proof enough, isn't it? You should try some. Do you good.' I shook my head. It looked revolting. 'Please yourself,' he said.

'It could've been the pills, couldn't it?' I ventured.

'Don't think so,' said Popsicle, smiling sheepishly. 'I haven't taken them, have I? Not one. Just pretended. Spat them out again. Don't like pills. Don't trust 'em. Give me my old condensed milk any day. I'll be right as rain now, in no time, you'll see.'

A sudden frown came over his face like a shadow.

He beckoned me closer, and gripped me by the arm. There was a wildness in his eyes that frightened me. 'Remember what I said, Cessie. Whatever happens, I don't ever want to go up to Shangri-La. Never, d'you hear me? Never.'

7 SHANGRI-LA

WHETHER IT WAS THE CONDENSED MILK OR NOT, Popsicle was certainly a changed man. He was using his bad arm more and more every day, so that I now had difficulty in remembering which arm was supposed to be the weaker of the two. No one cut his food up for him any more. No one tied his shoe-laces. He did everything for himself. He was still absent-minded occasionally; but he was much happier in himself, so much so that by the time term began the following Monday morning, we were confident enough to leave him on his own in the house for the day.

To my huge relief, school turned out not to be the nightmare I had been dreading – Shirley Watson was off sick, and she wouldn't be back for a couple of weeks at least. When I got back after school the house had been cleaned from top to bottom and tea was ready for me on the kitchen table.

'Marmite and hot buttered toast,' Popsicle said. 'Is that all right for you, madam?' And he sat me down, pushing my chair in behind me. Normally I would have come home to an empty house and my own company.

To her huge delight, my mother had the same waiter service when she came back from school, exhausted as usual. She could not believe what Popsicle had done around the house.

Every day that followed was the same. The garden, muddied and blackened by the fire, was slowly being restored, and he had set about the building of a new garden shed. In fine weather, the patio became his carpenter's shop. When it rained he used the garage. Within weeks the garden shed was up, much bigger and much better than it had ever been before.

One windy autumn afternoon we held an opening ceremony. My father was speechless as he cut the ribbon, and still speechless when we were allowed inside for the first time.

Popsicle, it seemed to me, was like a small boy out to impress his father – in this case my father – and my father was impressed, I could see he was. But he simply would not say so. All he said was, 'Lot of work gone into this, I should think. Looks sound; but don't go lighting fires too close, will you?' It was supposed to be a joke, I think, but it just wasn't funny.

By now it was as if Popsicle had always lived with us. He'd wash the cars on Sundays, put the rubbish out for the dustmen on Tuesday. He'd even help me with my French homework – so much about him was completely unexpected.

When I asked him once how it was that he knew so much French, he went strangely quiet on me. I should have known better than to ask. It was always the same. Any question that related in some way to his past he would deflect or simply ignore. He would sometimes talk wistfully about his years as a boatbuilder in Bradwell when he was a young father and a young husband, but that still seemed to be all he could remember – in spite of the condensed milk, which he took religiously every night. But at least his inability to remember did not seem to be lowering his spirits as it had before. No one was more chirpy about the house than Popsicle. He was the whistling outside in the garden and the singing up in the bathroom. He was the life and soul of the place.

Home was happier now than it ever had been, despite my father's continuing coolness towards Popsicle. And at school too life was proving unexpectedly good. Shirley Watson was back, but was ignoring me – so far. Things were set fair, I thought.

These days, I noticed, Popsicle would often disappear into the new garden shed and lock himself in for hours on end. I asked him time and again what he was doing in there. 'Tell you when I'm ready,' he'd say, tapping his nose conspiratorially. 'And you're not to peek.' I tried to peek of course, but he'd hung an old sack over the window. All I could see through a knot-hole low down in the door was a tray of onions on the floor. I was none the wiser.

20th of October. My twelfth birthday. It was a Saturday. When I came down there were three wrapped presents waiting for me on the kitchen table. Everyone was sitting there and singing happy birthday. I opened the cards first and then attacked the presents. I had a CD of Yehudi Menuhin playing Beethoven's Violin Concerto from my father, and from my mother a video of *The Black Stallion*, my favourite film in all the world. I left Popsicle's till last.

'Go careful,' he said, as I tore the paper away. It was a shoe box, but it wasn't shoes inside. It was a boat, a model boat, blue with a single yellow funnel. I took it out. It looked like some sort of a lifeboat, with looping ropes along the sides. Below the funnel a man stood at the huge steering-wheel. He was dressed in a yellow sou'wester and oils, and he really looked as if he was clinging to the wheel in the teeth of a gale. The name *Lucie Alice* was painted in red on the side of the boat.

I put it down very gently beside the Grape Nuts in the middle of the table. I looked at Popsicle. 'That was my boat,' he said proudly. 'The *Lucie Alice*.'

'Beautiful,' my mother breathed. 'Just beautiful.'

'You made it?' I said. 'In the shed?' Popsicle nodded.

'Built in 1939 she was. Served at Lowestoft for thirty years. Reserve boat down in Exmouth after that. Know every plank of her, every nail. Don't know why, but I do. She went to Dunkirk in 1940 too, in the war. Took hundreds of our lads off the beaches, she did.'

'Where is she now?' my father asked.

Popsicle got up suddenly from the table. 'How should I know?' he said. 'I just made it, that's all.' I went after him and caught him by the arm before he reached the door.

'It's lovely, Popsicle,' I said. 'Will it float? Can I float it in the bath, with Patsy?'

'In the bath! With Patsy!' he laughed. 'This is my lifeboat you're talking about.'

'All right then. What about the pond? Could we

float him out on the pond, in the park?'

'Not him,' he said. 'She's a she. All boats are shes. She'll float all right, but she'll do a lot more than just float, you mark my words. She's got engines. I've tried her out. She's had her sea trials. Goes like the clappers, she does. And she's unsinkable too. Got to be if she's a lifeboat. You want to see?'

'Now?'

'Why not? We'll all go, shall we?'

The ducks were not at all pleased with us. They must have thought we'd come over with our usual offering of breadcrusts. Popsicle ignored all their raucous clamour, started the engines and set her chugging off across the pond on her maiden voyage. Transfixed, we all stood there and watched her, until Popsicle said that one of us had better run across the other side to catch her before she ran aground and got herself stuck in the mud. My father raced round. He was there just in time.

'She looks such a brave little boat,' said my mother.

'She was,' Popsicle replied. 'Saved a lot of lives in her time.'

'You crewed on her, did you?' my mother was delving, prying, and I wished she wouldn't. 'So you were a lifeboat-man, then?' I expected Popsicle to clam up, but he didn't, not this time.

'I wish I knew.' He was looking out over the pond as he spoke. 'I know that she was mine once, that's all.' He put an arm round my shoulder. 'And now she's yours, Cessie, all yours. You'll take good care of her, won't you? Course, you can let your dad play with her from time to time.' He chuckled. 'Look at him. Just like he was. Always loved boats, did your dad.' My father was crouched down by the pond pointing the bow of the lifeboat right at us.

'Ready?' he called out.

'Ready,' said Popsicle.

My father released the boat and then stood up to watch, hands on hips. He was beaming like a little boy.

By now a dozen people or more had gathered around the pond to watch, Shirley Watson amongst them with her dog. Mandy Bethel was there too. The dog, a snuffling puggy-looking thing with pop eyes, yapped incessantly from the edge of the pond. That dog and Shirley Watson, I was thinking, they really suit each other.

'It's mine. My grandad made it,' I crowed. I knew as soon as I'd said it that I should have kept my mouth shut. The trouble was that I felt safe. Popsicle was nearby. My mother and father too. I felt suddenly brave, so I bragged on. 'It's called the *Lucie Alice*. It's got real engines. It's an exact replica of a 1939 lifeboat, a real one.'

'Kids' stuff, if you ask me,' Shirley Watson sneered.

'Well,' I said, still full of bravado, 'if you don't like it, you don't have to watch, do you?'

Mandy Bethel gaped. She could not believe what she was hearing. Neither could I. No one spoke like that to Shirley Watson, no one in her right mind.

Shirley Watson glared at me and stomped off in a fury. I knew, as I watched her go, that I had done something I would live to regret. I knew she was best not roused, not confronted, and I had done both. I knew there would be trouble.

I soon discovered that Shirley Watson was putting it about at school that I had a crazy grandfather back at home, a drifter, a tramp, who wore his hair in a ponytail and looked like a pirate. That I could ignore, but there was worse to come – just looks at first, then whispers.

Shirley Watson was spreading poison about Popsicle. She was telling everyone. He looked like a druggie, a weirdo. He was probably a dealer too, hanging around the park like he did. And she'd seen him talking to small children. It was a deliberate campaign of innuendo and gossip, and I hated her for it from the bottom of my heart.

The mud was sticking. People were treating me differently. Some would not speak to me at all. I wanted to rise above it, to face them down, to be brave. I wanted to go out with Popsicle as often as I could, and be seen with him, just to show them exactly what I thought of them. And to begin with I really did try. But every time I went out with Popsicle, I was looking over my shoulder, dreading seeing anyone from school.

Gradually my courage ebbed away, and I was cowed into staying at home. I had homework, it was raining, I had violin practice to do – any excuse to avoid bumping into that gaggle of sniggering tormentors in the park. I wasn't proud of myself.

Popsicle kept making minor adjustments to improve the *Lucie Alice*'s performance or her stability in the water. He had to test his refinements on the duckpond in the park. There wasn't anywhere else. Luckily, there were long periods when he didn't want to go there at all – whilst he was working on her on his bench in the garden shed. 'Any boatbuilder worth his salt can't be satisfied with getting it almost right,' he told me one day, as I watched him at work. 'He has to get it perfect. And I'm going to get this boat perfect for you, Cessie, perfect.'

It looked quite perfect enough for me already, but I

wasn't going to argue. I was more than happy to sit and watch him at work, and happier still not to have to venture out into the park. But I knew the day must come when he would want to test the *Lucie Alice* out on the water again, and that unless I had a ready excuse, I'd have to go with him, my heart in my mouth all the time.

One Sunday afternoon I was reading on my bed when he came into my room with his coat on, the *Lucie Alice* in the shoe box under his arm. 'She's ready,' he said.

'It's raining,' I told him.

'Only drizzling, Cessie girl,' he said. 'Come on.' I had no choice.

I knew that Sunday afternoon was always the most likely time to meet some of Shirley Watson's crowd in the park. They could be on their way down to the bus shelter, a favourite hang-out at weekends, particularly when it was raining. I was thinking about that as I followed him down the stairs. 'But I haven't done my violin practice,' I said, stopping where I was.

'It won't take us long,' said Popsicle, and I could see how disappointed he was at my reluctance.

My father had heard us from the sitting-room. 'She needs to practise,' he said. 'She won't get her Grade Six by playing with boats, will she?' There was no need to say it like that. I very nearly changed my mind, just to show solidarity with Popsicle. But I didn't. Instead, to my everlasting shame, I gave Popsicle my scarf and sent him off to the park on his own in the rain.

I went up to my room and pretended to practise, but of course my heart wasn't in it. I spent all the time excusing my excuse, rationalising my chickening out. I just couldn't concentrate. I kept thinking of Popsicle out there in the park, of what Shirley's cronies might say to him if they caught up with him, how bewildered he'd be, how hurt. Then, quite suddenly, I could picture him in my mind. I knew they were there, all around him, laughing at him, jeering.

I was down the stairs and out of the house before anyone could stop me. I could hear my father calling after me as I slammed the door.

The traffic lights turned red at the right moment. I dashed across the main road, past the library and the bus shelter, and into the park. I hurdled the children's play-ground fence and got a shrill rebuke from an angry mother seesawing her little girl, before I hurdled out again. I was almost there.

To my intense relief there was no chanting, no jeering, just a commotion of quacking. There was no one about, only the ducks – that was how it seemed at first. But then I saw that the ducks were not alone in their pond. Popsicle was standing waist-high in the water, with his back to me. I called to him and ran down to the water's edge. He didn't turn; I ran round so that he'd have to hear me, have to see me. He had something in his hand. There was debris floating in the water all around him. I knew in an instant what had happened. I ran into the water and waded out towards him. He was holding the bow of the lifeboat in one hand, the stern in the other. The yellow funnel was floating towards me. I picked it up. I saw the wheel just under the surface and retrieved it. I looked for the lifeboatman in the sou'wester, but he was gone.

'They just came,' he said. 'They were shouting things, horrible things. Then they threw stones, hundreds of them. They went on and on. I don't know why. I don't know why.'

Nothing I said would persuade him to come out of the pond. He had to stay, he said, until he'd picked up every last bit of her. Then my father was there, and my mother too, wading out towards us. They took an elbow each and, ignoring all his protestations, led him out of the pond. When I looked back, the ducks were moving in amongst the last of the flotsam, pecking at it, then discarding it and finally swimming away in disgust.

After the sinking of the *Lucie Alice* Popsicle went

downhill again fast. Dr Wickens said he wasn't seriously ill. He had a chest cold, that was all. But even I could see it was a lot more than that. He was sinking further and further into despair. Every day now was a black-dog day. He'd sit there in his chair, his eyes glazed, and unseeing. He wasn't with us. He seemed lost in a deep sadness and could not bring himself out of it. I told him it didn't matter about the *Luice Alice*, that he could always build another. I stroked his hand and told him we'd do it together. I think he barely knew I was there. He didn't feel like eating. He even refused his condensed milk.

The doctor came back one evening to give Popsicle an injection, just to help him along, I was told. I was sent upstairs for a while. They wanted to talk to the doctor in private. I heard the hushed discussions down in the kitchen, but the tap was running or the kettle was boiling and I could make no sense of what they were saying.

At school it took a few days to screw up my courage before I could bring myself to do what I had to do, to say what I had to say. Shirley Watson knew it was coming. There was guilt written all over her face. She couldn't hide it. Day in, day out, I had eyed her from across the classroom, from across the playground, just to let her know that I knew it was her that had sunk the *Lucie Alice*, her and her friends. At first she tried to stare me out, but each time I won the battle of the eyes, and she'd have to look away.

I waited for my moment. It came in break one day when I saw she was alone. I walked right up to her. We were face to face now. Somehow my courage held firm. 'Why? What did you do it for?' My voice was steadier than I dared hope. 'My grandad made me that boat. It took him weeks and weeks. What you did, it's made him ill, really ill. Does that make you feel good?' I looked her full in the eye, unflinching. 'Well, does it? Does it?' Then, without a word, she turned and ran off.

As I went home that afternoon I was singing inside with triumph. I told Popsicle all about how I'd faced down Shirley Watson. I wasn't sure how much he understood, but he seemed to listen. After I'd finished he just touched my face, and smiled wanly. 'Lucie Alice,' he said. 'Lucie Alice.' And that was all.

If there were warnings of what was about to happen, then I didn't see them. Perhaps I didn't want to see them. For a week or so over half-term, a nurse came each day to see to Popsicle, and the doctor was in and out almost daily too. I would see my mother and father walking around the garden, deep in earnest discussion from which I was always excluded. There would be long knowing looks across the table at supper, and my father, I noticed, was being unusually attentive and kind towards Popsicle.

I had just come home from school. I was hanging up my coat in the front hall. I remember thinking how odd it was that both cars were parked outside, that my father and my mother must both be home early. They were waiting for me as I walked into the kitchen. She should have been at school. He should have been at work. Something was definitely wrong.

'Where's Popsicle?' I said, dumping my bag on the floor.

'Sit down, Cessie,' said my father. 'We've got something to tell you.' Then he was looking across to my mother for help.

'It's Popsicle, Cessie.' She was trying to tell me something she didn't want to tell me. 'Don't worry, it's nothing terrible,' she went on. 'It's just that . . . just that we've had to send him away for a while. We can't cope with him here, not like he is. He wasn't taking his pills like he should. He was just getting worse. We had to do something.'

'What do you mean "send him away"?'

'Well . . .' she began, and she wouldn't look at me as she spoke. 'It's a sort of home for the elderly, a nursing home where he can be looked after properly. He'll have everything he needs.'

'Shangri-La,' said my father. 'It's called Shangri-La. Lovely place. He'll be fine there, Cessie. It's what's best for him, honestly it is.'

'Come to think of it,' my mother went on, 'Cessie was asking about Shangri-La only the other day, weren't you, Cessie? Funny that.'

There was nothing funny about it, nothing at all.

8 THE *LUCIE ALICE*

FOR DAYS I WOULDN'T SPEAK TO EITHER OF THEM.
As far as I was concerned they were both as guilty as
each other. I spent much of my time alone in my room
brooding over the dreadful thing they had done to
Popsicle. They would come up, sit on the bed and try to
talk me round. I had to understand that, at the moment,
Shangri-La was the best place for him, and it was a
perfectly nice place too. You couldn't hope for better.
But I was deaf to all explanations, all excuses.

'It won't be for ever, you know,' my mother told me.
'Just for a while, till he gets better.'

'Don't think badly of us, Cessie,' my father pleaded.
'I know how upset you must be, but what else could we
have done? The way he is, he needs proper full-time
care. I've got to go out to work. Your mother's got to go

out to work. You've got to go to school. We just couldn't leave him alone in the house, not as he is. Remember the fire? It's no use carrying on like this, you know. It won't achieve anything, Cessie. It won't bring Popsicle home.'

But it wasn't only the sending away of Popsicle that grieved me, nor even where he'd been sent – that wasn't their fault – it was how it had been done, covertly, on the sly. I wasn't stupid. I could understand that Popsicle shouldn't be left all on his own. I could even understand that in his state of mind he could possibly do himself some accidental damage. But they had packed him off to Shangri-La, to the very place Popsicle most dreaded, and without even telling me. I could have warned them. I could have told them.

On the principle that I would never again let them have the satisfaction of hearing me play my violin, I waited until I was sure I was alone in the house before I began my practice. I always ended with 'Nowhere Man', dedicating it each time to Popsicle, and promising him as I played that somehow I would get him out of Shangri-La. I could never play that tune without crying for him. It was while I was playing it one afternoon that I decided the time had come to stop moping, and to do what I should have done in the first place.

I packed away my violin and got my bike out of the back of the garage. If I was to rescue him, then I had to get to see him. The first step was to find out where the Shangri-La nursing home was. I asked a postman. 'Cliff Road,' he said, 'on the coast road, going west out of town, top of the hill.'

It turned out to be a long way out of town, beyond the harbour, beyond the marina, a couple of kilometres at least. The hill was horribly steep, but I was determined to keep pedalling right to the top. Once I reached it, I got off, gasping for breath, and rested. There it was across the road – 'Shangri-La. Residential Nursing Home for the Elderly'. Beyond the closed white gate was a driveway, and an avenue of trees, every one of them slanted and stunted by the wind. There were lawns and rhododendron bushes and, just visible from the road, a great gabled house, cream-painted with neat, white windows.

There didn't seem to be anyone about, so I opened the gate and wheeled my bike up the drive. The porch alone was as big as the front of our entire house. It had fluted pillars all around like a temple, and two stone lions glared at me from either side of the front door. I pressed the brass bell and stood back. I didn't think I was frightened but I could hear my heart pounding in my ears. No one came. I rang again. Still no one came. I wheeled my bike round the side of the house and peered in at the first window I came to.

They were sitting around the room, ancient men and ancient women, some with their heads lolling in sleep, their mouths wide open; others staring vacantly into space, their hands trembling in their laps. A few were reading magazines. One of them looked up at me, looked straight at me I thought, but she didn't see me.

It was a huge square room with a high ceiling and a chandelier. On the walls there were pictures in gold frames of cart horses and sailing boats and village feasts, and beneath them the room was lined with grey-green chairs with wooden armrests. A television was on in the corner, but no one seemed to be watching it.

I was searching amongst the faces for Popsicle, but I couldn't find him, not at first. Only when he stood up and came walking towards me across the room did I know him. His cheeks seemed sunken, his skin sallow. His hand was reaching out towards me.

'Cessie,' he mouthed.

A voice spoke from behind me. 'And what have we

here?' Her grey hair was as starched and stiff as her white uniform. She was a thin-lipped, peaky-faced woman with sharp little eyes. 'You do this often, do you, peering in people's windows?'

I ran for it across the lawn, leapt on my bike and was gone down the drive. I dismounted at the gate, fought with the latch that wouldn't budge, flung the gate back and at last made my escape. I never looked back, not once.

I wasn't going to give up. One way or another I had to see Popsicle. I had to talk to him, to tell him I hadn't been part of the conspiracy, that I'd known nothing at all about it. So that evening I broke my silence for the first time. 'I want to visit Popsicle,' I said. 'Even in prison you're allowed visits, aren't you?'

They seemed relieved that I was talking to them again.

'Soon,' said my mother. 'They said we should let him settle in for a while. But it's been two weeks now – we could go on Saturday, couldn't we, Arthur? What d'you think?'

'Why not?' my father replied, and then he smiled at me. 'Truce?'

'Truce,' I said, but I didn't mean it.

I had several long days at school to endure before Saturday. Word had got around that Popsicle was up at

Shangri-La. It seemed Mandy Bethel's aunt worked there as a part-time nurse. Ever since I had confronted Shirley Watson, she and Mandy Bethel and the others were giving me a wide berth – thank goodness. But there were some who felt they had to say something. They were meaning to be sympathetic, but sometimes it didn't come out like that. 'They're all really old up there.' 'Must be horrible for him – with all those wrinklies, I mean.' 'I've seen them out in their bus on outings. They look prehistoric, if you ask me.' And so on. I endured it as best I could, but it wasn't easy.

On the Friday morning, we had RE with Mrs Morecambe. It all got silly and out of hand, as it often did with Mrs Morecambe. Her crowd control was never much good, but at least she was always interesting. She was talking about Hinduism, about the transmigration of souls. Some people saw this as an opportunity to wind her up by suggesting what they'd most like to be when they came back in their next life. There were all sorts of ridiculous ideas: elephants, kangaroos, dung-beetles, daddy-long-legs, even a flea. Finally she'd had enough. She banged the table. 'It is not a joking matter,' she stormed, her eyes flashing. 'It's about time some of you learnt that life is not one long joke, and nor is death either.' There was still some tittering. 'You won't think it's so funny when your time comes, and it will come. It comes to us all. I've got an aunt. She's up at the Shangri-La nursing home right now. And she won't ever come out. Just sixty. Been there five years now. Alzheimer's. She can't feed herself. Some days she doesn't even know who she is any more. She hasn't known me for two years.' Suddenly everyone was looking at me. Mrs Morecambe went on: 'Believe you me, getting old is no laughing matter.' No one was laughing any more.

Mrs Morecambe called me up after the lesson. 'It's not too bad up at Shangri-La, Cessie. They do what they can,' she said. So she knew too. 'Don't let it worry you.' It was kind of her, but it was no comfort to me. The memory of Popsicle's pained face through the window haunted me night and day. His worst nightmare had come true, and I was to blame, in part at least. I had promised him he would never have to go to Shangri-La, and I had broken that promise. Somehow I would get him out of there. Somehow.

I thought about little else. I had the notion that Popsicle and I could steal away together in the middle of the night and make our way down to the railway station. We'd catch the first train out in the morning – it didn't matter where it was going. I had nearly a hundred pounds in the building society, enough to take us a long way away. He could make ship models, and we could sell them. I'd look after him. He'd be fine. We'd both be fine. We'd find a house somewhere remote, somewhere no one would even think of looking for us.

I knew all along that it was a dream, but I clung to it all the same, and just hoped that there was some way I could make at least some of it come true.

I was still hoping, still dreaming as we drove up to Shangri-La that Saturday morning. We turned in off the road and up the drive. 'See?' my mother was saying. 'We told you, Cessie. Isn't it lovely? Wonderful views, rose gardens. They've got croquet too, look. And you should see inside. Library. Television room. Carpets everywhere. Paradise on a hill. Lovely views of the harbour. They don't call it Shangri-La for nothing.'

We weren't the only people visiting. Half a dozen cars were parked on the front drive, and on the front lawn they were playing croquet, with a couple of little children jumping the hoops as if they were hurdles.

'Our future Olympic champions perhaps, Mr Stevens,' said a voice from behind me, a voice I recognised at once. Striding across the drive was the starched lady in the white uniform whom I'd met on my previous visit, the lady with the sharp little eyes and the thin lips. I tried to hide behind my mother.

'I heard your programme yesterday evening, Mr Stevens. Excellent as usual, quite excellent. And who is this then?'

'This is Cessie, Popsicle's granddaughter,' said my mother, stepping aside so that I was now completely exposed. 'Cessie, this is Mrs Davidson. She's the matron here, and she's looking after Popsicle for us.' I need not have worried about being recognised. Mrs Davidson wasn't interested in me. She was soon deep in discussion with my mother and father. They'd forgotten all about me.

'It's early days,' Mrs Davidson was saying, 'but your father's making very good progress already, Mr Stevens. He can be a bit cantankerous, of course, but we're used to that at Shangri-La. He still won't take his pills, but there we are. You can lead a horse to water . . .'

'But is he eating better now?' my mother asked.

They had all turned away from me and were walking towards the house. I took my chance and made off. I had it in mind that I would find Popsicle before they did and tell him of my plans for his escape. He had to know that I hadn't abandoned him, and that I never would.

I must have been preoccupied. I was making my way across the lawn, past the rose garden towards the window where I'd seen Popsicle before, when I walked right into a man in a wheelchair.

'Where you off to in such a hurry, young lady?' I expected him to be furious, but he wasn't. 'Visiting someone, are you?'

'I'm looking for Popsicle, for my grandad,' I said.

When he smiled I saw he had very even, very yellow teeth. He held out his hand. 'I'm Harry,' he said, 'and you must be Cessie. Never stops talking about you. Pretty as a picture, just like he said you were. Grand fellow, your grandad. Won't stand any nonsense from the Dragon-woman.' I knew well enough who he was talking about. He looked around him and then beckoned me closer. 'All smiles she is on visiting days. Different story when they've gone. Shouts at us like we're all deaf. Treats us like we're a bunch of loonies. I'm telling you. It's not right what she does. Not right at all. Popsicle – he's the only one that talks back at her. And she doesn't like it, not one bit. Got it in for him already, she has, but Popsicle doesn't take no notice.'

'Where is he?' I asked.

'He goes down to the gun emplacement on the cliffs. Just sits there, looking at the boats going in and out, birdwatching sometimes, or reading his poetry. Potty about poetry, isn't he? Best place to think his thoughts, he says.' He pointed through the trees. 'Over there he doesn't like to be disturbed. But he won't mind, not if it's you.' I began to move away, but he hadn't finished yet. 'I'll tell you something else, young lady. He may not have been here long, but your grandad, he's like a breath of fresh air. Keeps us smiling, he does. And that's a lot to be thankful for. Off you go now.'

I found Popsicle standing on top of a concrete bunker. There were holes in the sides where I supposed the guns had once been. He was looking out to sea through a pair of binoculars. He hadn't heard me, so I climbed up behind him and tapped him on the shoulder. The moment he saw me his face lit up.

He hugged me to him tight for a moment or two, and then held me at arm's length. He seemed so much happier than the last time I'd seen him, more his old self again. 'Oh, Cessie, I've been hoping you'd come back. Every day I've been hoping. That woman, that Dragon-woman, she didn't catch you when you came before? She didn't catch you?' I shook my head. I had everything ready to tell him, my whole escape plan, but I didn't get the chance even to begin. 'Good, good. Now listen, Cessie. I've got news for you, good news. I've remembered something, something important. That boat I made you, it's more than just a boat.'

'What d'you mean?'

His eyes shone with excitement. 'It's where I live, Cessie. It's my home. That boat's my home. I live on the *Lucie Alice*.' I must have looked a bit doubtful. 'It's true, Cessie. I live on that boat. Honestly. I woke up a couple of days ago and I just knew it. Don't ask me how. I reckon it's the old memory waking himself up at last. About time too, if you ask me. It's just like the one I made you, the one they went and sunk. I'm not barmy, Cessie, honestly I'm not. For a while I really thought I was, and it frightened the living daylights out of me. You do believe me, don't you?'

'Of course I do,' I said, but I wasn't at all sure that I did. I had to ask: 'But where is it then? Where you live, the boat, where is it?'

He looked suddenly downcast. 'That's the thing, Cessie. That's the bit I don't know. I mean, it's got to be moored somewhere, hasn't it? I'm still trying to work it out, and I will too. I will. You'll see.'

A pair of gulls wheeled above our heads and flew out to sea. 'Lesser Blackbacks,' he said. 'Have a look.' He took off his binoculars and gave them to me. It was a few moments before I had them in focus. I found them floating out on the thermals over the cliffs. 'That's what I'd like to be, free as they are,' said Popsicle. 'All my life

106

there's one thing I've hated, Cessie. You know what it is? Being cooped up, shut in, told what to do. That's why I always dreaded coming up here to Shangri-La. I heard all about it from a friend of mine – Sam he's called. Sam had an older brother, and he went a bit barmy in the head. So Sam had to send him up here to be looked after. He hated it up here, and he never came out. That's not going to happen to me, Cessie. I'm getting out of here, soon as ever I can.' He was angry now, angrier than I'd ever seen him. 'There's fine people in this place, good people, but that Mrs Davidson, that Dragon-woman, she who must be obeyed, I've seen her scream-ing at them, Cessie. Maybe we're a bit slow. Maybe some of us wet ourselves. But that's not our fault, is it? And all she does is scream at us. Not right, Cessie, not fair. Little Hitler she is. I'm telling you, Cessie, I'm getting out – and for two pins I'd take Harry and the others with me. Honest I would. Soon as I remember where that boat of mine is, I'll be gone, out of here for good.'

That was when I heard my mother's voice from in amongst the trees.

'Popsicle!' She was hurrying down towards us, and with her were Mrs Davidson and my father.

'We've been looking for you, Mr Stevens. I thought

107

I told you to stay inside to meet your visitors, in the dayroom,' said Mrs Davidson. There was an edge to her voice that hadn't been there before.

'How are you, Popsicle?' My mother was helping Popsicle down off the gun emplacement. 'Mrs Davidson says you're eating really well these days. That's good, very good.' She breathed deep of the air as she looked out to sea. 'Isn't this the perfect place?'

'You doing all right, then?' my father asked.

'Better all the time, Arthur. And d'ya know why? I was telling Cessie. I've remembered. I've remembered where I live. It's on the *Lucie Alice*.' They were all looking at him, nonplussed. 'That's right. It's a boat, just like the one I made for Cessie. It's a lifeboat, and I live on it.'

We didn't stay talking for very long. Popsicle did his best to explain how it was that he could be so sure about the *Lucie Alice*; but how, even so, he still couldn't remember where it was moored. 'That'll come,' he said. 'That'll come.' But I could see what Popsicle couldn't see, that they all thought he was losing his mind, that Shangri-La was just where he should be, and where he'd have to stay.

All the while Mrs Davidson was eyeing me. I was sure she was beginning to recognise me.

As we were leaving she took Popsicle by the elbow.

'I think you'd better come inside now, Mr Stevens, don't you? Bit breezy out here.'

'I'll be fine where I am,' Popsicle pulled away. 'I like a good breeze. Gets rid of bad smells, if you know what I mean.' Mrs Davidson glared at him.

When we said goodbye I held him as long and as tight as I could, so that he'd remember it when I was gone. It was all I could do to choke back my tears. 'Don't you go crying on me, girl,' he whispered. 'I've got enough on my plate without that.'

My mother kissed him goodbye too. 'It's not for ever Popsicle,' she said. 'You do understand that. Just till you're better. We'll come again soon.'

My father shook Popsicle by the hand. There was just a nod between them and a brief meeting of eyes.

'You do see what I mean,' said Mrs Davidson as we walked away. 'He says such bizarre things. He does live in a bit of a fantasy world, I'm afraid, but he'll settle down. They all take time to settle. I'll look after him, don't you worry.' To me, that sounded more like a threat than anything else.

We drove home in silence. I waited till the engine was turned off before I let them both know exactly what I was thinking. 'I don't know how you can do it, how you can leave him up there in that place with that horrible woman.' They stayed silent, which simply provoked me to go further. 'You don't believe him, do you? You never do. If he says he lives on a lifeboat, then he does. Why should he make it up? You think he's mad, do you? Well, you're the mad ones. Why don't you just trust him? Why don't you ever trust him?'

I lay there that night asking myself that very same question. Try as I did to dispel them, my doubts still nagged at me. Was Popsicle really in his right mind? How could he be living on a lifeboat? If I could find the *Lucie Alice*, if only I could prove there was such a boat . . . I knew what I had to do. I don't think I slept at all.

I was up early. I told them I was going for a cycle ride. I searched the marina from end to end, and the harbour beyond. There was no lifeboat. I went out after lunch and tried again. There was no *Lucie Alice*. No one had ever heard of her. So maybe they were right after all. Maybe Popsicle *was* sick in his head. Maybe he was barmy. I remembered what Mrs Morecambe had said about her aunt in the RE lesson, how she was dying of Alzheimer's. I went and looked up Alzheimer's in a medical dictionary from my mother's bookshelf. It took me some time to find it, because I didn't know how to spell it. Everything I read confirmed my worst fears. Alzheimer's began with muddled thinking, with intermittent loss of memory. When I'd finished reading I was quite sure that Popsicle was in the early stages of Alzheimer's.

With two sleepless nights behind me, I was so tired the next day and so worried that I could hardly think straight at all. The last person in the world I wanted to have to face at school was Shirley Watson. I was sitting under a tree eating my lunch on my own, when I looked up and saw her coming towards me. There was nothing I could do to avoid her. She stood for a moment looking down at me out of the sun. I thought she was going to kick my head in.

'You know that boat?' Her tone was conciliatory, ingratiating almost. 'Well, I've seen it,' she said.

'What do you mean, you've seen it? You bust it up, remember?'

'No, I mean a big one, a real one. Down by the canal. By the lock. You been there?' I shook my head. 'I was fishing down there yesterday with my brother. There's a whole lot of barges moored down by the old warehouses, and right at the end there's this boat, and it's just like the one your grandad made. Just the same it is. I'm not having you on, Cessie, promise. It's there, really

111

there. "*Lucie* . . ." something or other, it's called. Great big yellow funnel. Blue, just like the one . . .' She was shifting nervously from one foot to the other. 'I'll show you, if you like. After school?'

9 GONE MISSING

IT WAS A LONG WALK FROM SCHOOL TO THE canal, right across the other side of town. All the way I felt uneasy. Shirley Watson didn't say very much. There was never a mention of the sinking of the *Lucie Alice*. She asked after Popsicle, and she seemed genuinely concerned, as if she really cared about him. It wasn't like her at all. All the while I felt I might be being led into some kind of a trap. I stayed with her only because I knew there had to be some truth in her story. No one else could possibly have known what Popsicle had told me up at Shangri-La, about the *Lucie Alice*. She couldn't have plucked the idea out of thin air. But Shirley Watson was Shirley Watson, so I stayed on my guard.

As we neared the lock gates I was becoming ever more intrigued, but ever more anxious too. She stopped on the bridge and pointed. 'There. See?' I could see only the funnel at first, a yellow funnel beyond the line of brightly painted pleasure barges. But then I saw the side of the boat, dark blue, broader than the barges, her hull bellying out into the canal, a rope looping the length of her, just as there had been on the model Popsicle had made me. I looked around nervously, half expecting some kind of an ambush.

'What's the matter?' Shirley Watson asked.

'You,' I said. And then I asked her straight. 'What are you doing this for? Why did you bring me?'

I didn't know Shirley Watson could cry, but suddenly there were real tears in her eyes. 'What happened to your grandad, I didn't mean it to happen like it did. It just got out of hand. I don't know why we did it, and I wish . . .' She couldn't say any more. She turned away and went off, leaving me alone by the canal.

As I walked over the bridge it was coming on to rain. I hurried along the towpath past the barges – they had names like *Kontiki* and *Hispaniola* – and there in front of one was the vertical prow of the lifeboat rising majestically from the water, her name painted in large red letters on her side: *Lucie Alice*. I stepped over the mooring ropes and ran my hand along her side. She felt so solid, so sturdy.

The towpath in front of me and behind me looked deserted, and so it seemed was the boat. I called out. 'Anyone there? Anyone on board?' Then I saw the huge wheel – polished wood and brass – as high as a man, and beyond it the dark of the cabin down below. The only difference between this boat and Popsicle's model, apart from size of course, was that no man stood at the wheel in his sou'wester. In every other detail this was the same boat. I called out once more just to be sure. There was no reply, and there was no one watching except a pair of swans gliding past on the canal. It looked safe enough for me to go on board.

For a few moments I stood at the wheel and just held it. It wasn't hard to imagine the towering seas and the throb of the engines and the cries of the shipwrecked sailors. I could almost feel the spray on my face and the cruel wind whipping the seas into a frenzy all around me. I clung to the wheel now for dear life, just like the man in the sou'wester. I looked up at the funnel, but the rain stung my eyes at once so I had to look away. There was a gangway of some kind leading down, to the cabin perhaps, or to the engine-room.

In the oily darkness below decks it was difficult at first to make things out. I could see the shapes of two bulky engines amidships, and beyond them a small door with a brass handle. I tried to open it, but it was locked firmly. I turned the handle again and shook it. I put my shoulder to the door and pushed. It wouldn't give. Only then did it occur to me that I was trespassing, and more serious still, that I could be caught trespassing.

The boat breathed and groaned around me like a living thing, as if she knew I was an intruder and was telling me exactly what she thought of me. My eyes were becoming more accustomed to the dark now, and I saw to my left, down a small flight of steps, what looked like a ship's galley – a small sink, a worktop, a gas ring. There was a bottle of washing-up liquid on the shelf, and a couple of saucepans and a frying-pan hanging up on hooks above the sink. Everything was very tidy and in its place.

I was reaching out to try the tap, to see if it worked, when I heard a footfall on the deck right above my head.

'Come on up, whoever you are.' A man's voice and it was not friendly. 'I know you're down there.' I thought of hiding down there in the dark, but I knew there was no point. I had nowhere to run to. Sooner or later he'd find me. I had no choice. I climbed up into the glare of the daylight.

He had a sailor's peaked cap on the back of his head and wore a navy blue sweater that was full of holes. He was pointing his pipe at me as if it was a weapon.

'And what the blazes do you think you're doing down there?' My mind was racing. I knew how guilty I must have looked. 'Vandal, are you? One of those vandals?'

'No,' was all I could manage.

'What then? It's private property this. You can't just go snooping about on private property whenever you feel like it. All the same these days, you young ones. Think you can do what you please. Well you can't, not on my patch. I'm the lock-keeper. I look after all the canal moorings. My job. This boat belongs to a friend of mine, and a good friend too. Done it up himself. Pride and joy of his life it is.'

'My grandad,' I said. Gulls screamed overhead and suddenly I could see how it all fitted. 'He's my grandad.' Everything Popsicle had said all along had been true. He *could* see the water from his windows. There *were* ducks on the canal, and gulls *were* always screaming around his house. His house *was* the boat, and the boat *was* called the *Lucie Alice*, all just as he'd said.

'This grandad of yours,' the lock-keeper went on, and I could tell from his tone he didn't believe me, 'what's his name then?'

'Stevens. Same name as me. But we call him Popsicle. Everyone does.' He seemed taken aback, disappointed almost. I went on: 'And he's got long, yellow hair and it's tied back in a ponytail.' The lock-keeper took a moment or two to recover.

'He really is your grandad then?' I nodded. 'Didn't know he had any family. Is he all right? I haven't seen him down here for ages. Must be a couple of months now at least. I know he's always going off on his wanders; but he's been gone a long time. I was getting worried.'

'He's been ill. He's been staying with us,' I said.

'Not serious, is it?'

'No, he's better now, thanks. Trouble is . . .' I said, inventing hard as I went along. 'He wants me to fetch some things from the boat for him. But he never told me where he keeps the key to the cabin. It's locked.'

The lock-keeper smiled at me, and I knew then that I'd won him over. 'That's easy; and what with you being his relation, like you say, I don't suppose he'd mind me telling you, would he? In the galley. He keeps it in the tea-tin under the sink. You tell him Sam sends his best, will you?'

'You're Sam?' I asked.

'That's me,' he said. 'He's told you about me, has he?'

So this was the friend Popsicle had spoken of, the friend whose brother had been taken off up to Shangri-La, never to come out again.

'Popsicle, he'll be coming back soon, will he?' said the lock-keeper.

'Very soon,' I replied.

'Good,' he said. 'You take care now.' And he was gone.

I found the key in the tea-tin just where he'd said. The cabin door unlocked easily and I stepped inside. It was a whole house in one long room. The floor was strewn with overlapping rugs, all of them threadbare. His bed was at the far end, a radio on his bedside table. There were three armchairs grouped under a single oil-lamp which hung from the ceiling in the middle of the cabin, and the walls were stacked high with books all around. Huge though the cabin was – the full width of the lifeboat and half its entire length I guessed – it was somehow still snug and homely.

To one side of me was a writing-desk covered with charts, a pair of binoculars and a photograph in a frame. I walked round the desk and sat down. I noticed then that not all of the books were in English. Some were in French. On every ledge and shelf where there weren't books, there were models of ships: fishing smacks, clippers, super-tankers and dozens of different yachts. Across the cabin, opposite me was a workbench under the roof light. An unfinished model of what looked like a warship lay on its side, a chisel nearby, and a squeezed-out tube of glue; and there were pieces of used sandpaper scattered all over the place.

I turned the photograph into the light so I could see it better. It was of my father. It was a photo with his printed signature on it, the one he gives away to his fans when they write in. I didn't like him smiling at me, so I looked away. That was when I first noticed the wall behind Popsicle's bed, in the darkest corner of the cabin. It was covered with a collage of newspaper cuttings. I knelt up on the bed to get a closer look. The biggest cutting was a photograph of a beach, a wide beach stretching away into the distance, with high dunes behind and plumes of black smoke rising from a town in the background. In the foreground there were long lines of men in the sea, soldiers in helmets, some with rifles held above their heads. Another photograph was of a lifeboat crammed from end to end with soldiers, a lifeboat with a funnel amidships and a bow that rose vertically from the water.

The headline above it read: *Dunkirk. Lowestoft lifeboat rescues hundreds*. I could just about read the story below:

The Michael Hardy *of Lowestoft was one of sixteen lifeboats that took part in the recent heroic evacuation of the British Expeditionary Force from Dunkirk.*

*Along with hundreds of other small ships, she went in
and took the troops off the beaches, ferrying them to
bigger ships standing offshore outside the harbour.
Bombed and strafed continuously, the* Michael Hardy
*went back and forth for two nights and two days. She
was twice rammed in the darkness by German motor
torpedo boats but returned under her own steam to
Lowestoft, her brave work accomplished.*

There were several more articles like it, all with
photographs. Some were of ships sinking, some of
soldiers trooping wearily off ships. Others were of
soldiers with their hands on their heads being marched
away into captivity. Then I saw, right in the middle of
this collage of war, a tiny sepia photograph – the only
one that wasn't a newspaper photograph – of a young
woman standing in front of a town house. She was
laughing into the camera. She was pushing her hair
back out of her eyes. I unpinned it and took it to the
light. Something was written on the back of it. *Lucie
Alice. Dunkerque 1940. Pour toujours*. The writing was
faded but just legible.

I sat for a long time in the half dark of the cabin with
the photograph of Lucie Alice on Popsicle's desk in front
of me, trying to make sense of it all. By the time I left,

taking with me the photo of Lucie Alice and one of the newspaper cuttings, both pressed flat inside my English book, I had solved very little. This lifeboat, the one I was on, had been at Dunkirk – that was very evident. It looked exactly the same as the one in the newspaper cuttings. Then she had been called the *Michael Hardy*, and now she was the *Lucie Alice*, no doubt after the girl in the photo. But why the change? I stood on the towpath and looked up at the lifeboat. She was massive – I wondered how many soldiers she had carried out at a time, 200? 300? Popsicle must have been there. Had he been one of the soldiers rescued from the beaches perhaps? Or had he been a sailor on the *Michael Hardy*? And who was this Lucie Alice anyway? What did *pour toujours* mean? Was it Lucie Alice who had taught him French? Was that how Popsicle knew so much French?

As I walked home in the drizzle, my head reeling with unanswered questions, it occurred to me that, for the moment at least, I probably knew more about Popsicle's past than he did.

I was home late, very late. They'd both been out of their minds with worry, they told me. They had been ringing everywhere to find out where I was. 'I've just been for a walk,' I said. 'That's all.'

'That's all!' My father lost all patience. He glared at

me for a while, and then stormed out, leaving me with my mother in the kitchen.

'Why do you do these things, Cessie?' she said, shaking her head sadly. 'No one minds you going out for a walk, but you should've told us.'

'Like you told me about sending Popsicle to Shangri-La, I suppose,' I retorted.

I could see that she too was at the end of her tether. 'That was different. You know it was. I can't talk to you when you're like this. I've got some marking to do.'

I helped myself to a yoghurt from the fridge and sat down to think things through. I couldn't just leave it until visiting day the next Saturday to tell Popsicle of my discovery. The sooner he knew I'd found the *Lucie Alice*, the sooner he saw the photograph of Lucie Alice and the newspaper cutting, the sooner he might remember the rest. And, besides, I was burning to tell him. Perhaps, with these new pieces of the jigsaw puzzle in place, he might be able to put the whole picture together at last. I would cut school tomorrow and go up to Shangri-La. I'd forge a sick note and take it in the following day. Other people had done it and got away with it. No one would find out, not if I was careful. And I would be very careful.

Playing truant was not nearly as easy as I had

imagined. I left home at the normal time. That was a mistake for a start. I had planned to double back, wait for my mother and father to leave, take my bicycle from the garage and cycle up to Shangri-La. But I had forgotten something: on the way to school in the mornings, you were never alone, you were always one of a crowd.

Mandy Bethel was there, as usual. So were all the Martins from across the road, and then Shirley Watson and a dozen others joined us too. We were all of us walking to school, not necessarily together, but we were all going the same way. I couldn't just double back, not without questions being asked anyway.

I was almost at the park gates before I finally worked out something that had a chance of being believed. I stopped dead and pretended to search frantically in my bag. As she came past, Shirley Watson asked just the right question.

'Forgotten something?' She stopped beside me.

'Maths homework,' I replied.

'It *was* the same one, wasn't it?' she asked.

'What?' I couldn't think what she was talking about.

'That boat, that old boat on the canal.'

'Oh, that . . . Yes . . . Thanks . . . I'd better go back home and fetch it . . . I'll catch you up.' I ran off back across the road and into the estate without ever once looking behind me. I wasn't sure I'd been entirely convincing, but at least I'd got away.

I skulked in a bus shelter for a while, just until I was quite sure the house would be empty, and it was just as well I did. I'd been there only a few minutes when I saw my mother coming along the road in her car. I looked the other way hard, and hoped. Fortunately, she went by without seeing me. At least now I knew the coast was clear.

After that it was plain-sailing, except that the hill up to Shangri-La seemed a lot steeper and a lot longer than before. In the end I had to get off and walk, which was just as well because it gave me time to think. I couldn't just walk in there and announce that I wanted to see Popsicle. That Mrs Davidson, the Dragonwoman, would be bound to ask searching questions. I was in school uniform. Why wasn't I at school? I was alone. Where were my parents? At all costs I was going to have to avoid the Dragonwoman.

I left my bicycle hidden deep in the rhododendron bushes beside the drive, and then crawled the rest of the way through the undergrowth, until I was as close to the house as I dared. A white minibus was parked outside the pillared porch. I could just make out the writing on its side, in large pink lettering: 'Shangri-La. Residential Nursing Home'. I thought of making a dash for it, across the drive to the dayroom window overlooking the front lawn. It wasn't far, but I just couldn't summon up the courage to do it. I could see people moving about inside the house, but they were too far away, too shadowy for me to be able to identify any of them as Popsicle.

Then I had a stroke of luck. I'd been sitting there in the bushes for some time, wracked by indecision, hugging myself against the cold of the wind and with terrible pins and needles in my legs, when the front door opened. It was Harry, in his wheelchair. He was wheeling himself out from the shadow of the porch towards the rose garden on the other side of the drive from me. He had some kind of basket on his lap, a gardening trug perhaps. It crossed my mind that this might be the moment to make my move. The front door was open and inviting, and Harry would know where Popsicle was. It was a very good thing that caution got the better of me.

Suddenly Mrs Davidson was at the door and shouting after him. 'Half an hour only, Mr Mason. Do you hear me?'

Harry ignored her and went on wheeling.

The front door closed. Harry was bumping himself up on to the lawn. He reached the rose garden, took a pair of secateurs out of his trug and began clipping. I watched him, cowering in the undergrowth, and wondered what to do next.

'Cessie!' He wasn't looking at me, but it was Harry's voice – I was sure of it. 'Cessie! Don't say anything, and whatever you do, don't move. If I spotted you, then she could too. If you want to play hide-and-seek in dark green bushes then you shouldn't go wearing a red blazer – if you understand my meaning. I don't know what you're up to, young lady, but my guess is you've bunked off school to come and see your Popsicle. That right? Well you can't, not this morning. He didn't like the scrambled egg at breakfast, and he said so. She didn't like that, so she's gated him. He's got to stay in his room till lunch.'

'But I must see him. I've got something for him,' I said. 'It's important. It's really important.'

'All right, Cessie. Here's what I'm going to do. I'll clip off a few more of these deadheads, then I'll come over your side of the drive and park myself as close as I can. Give me a few moments. But don't move. Don't move a muscle.'

He clipped a last deadhead, glanced up casually at

the house, and then came wheeling across the drive towards me. There was a single rosebush in the centre of a small flower-bed. He stopped beside it with his back to me, so that he was between me and the house, and put his brake on. Then he reached out, caught a bloom between his fingers and pulled it gently to his nose.

'Old Velvet Tuscany,' he said, sniffing deeply and savouring it. 'Lovely old-fashioned rose. Scent of paradise. Beautiful. All right, so what do you want me to do then?'

'Tell him,' I was speaking as loudly as I dared. 'Tell Popsicle I've found his boat, I've found his home. It's down on the canal, by the barges. I've been there. And it *is* called the *Lucie Alice*, just like he said it was. And I found things, all sorts of things, photos, newspaper cuttings, all about the war, about the boat. I've got one or two of them with me. If he sees them, then maybe it'll help him remember. He fell over. He hit his head, lost his memory. But it's coming back, and this'll help, I know it will.'

'He's told us, Cessie,' Harry said. 'He told us everything, everything he can remember, that is. He'll be happy as pie about this, over the moon. Be a real fillip. It gets him down a bit sometimes, you know, when he can't remember. Thinks he's going barmy, round the twist; but he isn't, not our Popsicle. Don't you worry, Cessie, he's amongst friends up here. We've most of us got dicky memories, including me. Popsicle's no nutter. The Dragonwoman thinks he is, of course, but then she thinks we're all nutters. Where are the photos then?'

'In my bag. In my English book.'

'Now listen, Cessie, and listen good. You put it down, right where you are, and then get out of here, quick, before anyone spots you. I'll see he gets it, don't you worry.' I took out my English book and checked the cutting and the photo were still there. They were. I left it on the ground under the rhododendrons, backed away slowly on my hands and knees, retrieved my bicycle, jumped on, and made off like a bat out of hell.

For the rest of the day I loafed about the house behind closed curtains, worrying that some busybody might have seen me coming home from school in the morning, that someone might say something to my mother. I thought of playing my violin, but I couldn't, in case I was heard. In the end I went up to my room and finished my maths homework, and then read my book – *Animal Farm* it was.

When my mother came in, I played the exhausted schoolgirl and complained, bitterly and very convincingly I thought, about all the homework I'd been given that day. She wasn't at all sympathetic, but then I didn't expect her to be. I wasn't exactly in her good books. 'Then you'd better get on with it, hadn't you?' she said.

So it was that I found myself up in my room again doing more homework, or pretending to. I was still there when I heard my father come home. I didn't go down. I heard their confidential murmuring downstairs in the kitchen. They'd be talking about me, I was sure of it. I knelt down and put my ear to the floor. I was right.

'She'll get over it in time,' my mother was saying. 'You've got to remember, she's twelve; and believe you me, that's an awkward age for any girl. All right, so she's being a pain, a real pain; but when all's said and done, you can't blame her.'

'So you're blaming me then, I suppose?'

'No, I'm not blaming you either, nor Popsicle, nor anyone. We took a decision that was maybe the most difficult decision we've ever had to take. You didn't enjoy sending your father up there to that place, and neither did I. But it was the only thing we could do. You know something, Arthur? I hate myself for what we've done, and what's more I think you do too. And if we hate ourselves for sending him off to that place like we did, then we can hardly blame her for hating us too, can we? She loves that old man, and we sent him away. For God's sake, how do you expect her to feel?'

The doorbell rang. I heard my father leave the kitchen and go out into the hallway. I crept out on to the landing so that I could hear better. The door opened.

'Yes?' my father was saying.

'Is Cessie in?' It was Shirley Watson. She'd never ever called at my place before.

'She's upstairs.' My mother's voice.

'So she's all right then?'

'Yes, of course. Why do you ask?'

'Well . . .' Shirley began, and a cold shiver went up my spine. I knew already what she was about to say. 'Well, it's just that we were on our way to school this morning, and she forgot her homework and she went back to fetch it, and then she never came to school. I looked for her everywhere. Thought something might have happened to her that's all, but if she's here . . .' She knew then that she'd dropped me in it. To be fair to her, she did try to put it right, but it was too late. 'Well, maybe . . . maybe she wasn't feeling well or something.'

'Probably,' said my father, and I could sense the fury in him rising already.

'That's all right then,' said Shirley Watson. 'I'd better be going. I'll see her tomorrow. Bye.' The door closed.

'Cessie!' my father bellowed up the stairs. 'Get down here this minute. This minute!'

I appeared at the top of the stairs and came down slowly. I had no wish to hurry. They stood there in the hallway watching me. They waited until I was halfway down, until I was in range, before they began.

'How could you, Cessie?' said my mother. She was going to try the patient teacher approach. 'Where were you? Why? Why would you do such a thing?' I stayed inside myself, behind my wall of defiance. I would offer no explanations, no apologies, nothing.

'You go on like this, Cessie.' It was my father this time, stabbing his finger at me and fast losing all control. 'You go on like this and we're going to have to take steps, d'you hear me?' How could I not? He was shouting at the top of his voice, not two metres away.

'Leave it, Arthur,' my mother was trying again. 'I'll talk to her. Just leave it to me.' She came towards me. 'Is it something at school, Cessie? Are you in trouble? Has someone been bullying you, is that it?' She put her hand on mine on the banister. I pulled my hand away. 'This isn't like you, Cessie. How can we help you if we don't know what the problem is?' She looked deep into me and I did not flinch from her gaze. 'It isn't school at all, is it? This is a protest for Popsicle, isn't it? You stayed away from school to get back at us, didn't you? That's it, isn't it?'

My father was about to wade in again, but the phone rang and cut him off short. My mother picked it up. 'Mrs Davidson . . .?' The Dragonwoman. She'd seen me up at Shangri-La and was reporting it. I sat down on the stairs and prepared myself for the worst. 'When was this?' my mother was asking.

'What is it?' my father tried to interrupt. She shushed him, but he went on in spite of her. 'Is he all right? Is he ill?'

She put her hand over the mouthpiece and shook her head. 'No, it's not that. He's gone missing. Popsicle's gone missing. They haven't seen him since just after lunch. No one has. They've looked everywhere.'

Not quite everywhere, I thought, trying to hide my joy as best I could. Not quite everywhere.

10 DUNKIRK

THEY WERE GOING UP TO SHANGRI-LA RIGHT AWAY, they said, to see Mrs Davidson. I was to stay behind just in case Popsicle decided to come home in the meantime, and I had to be sure to call them at Shangri-La if he did. They were full of last-minute panicky instructions as they went out of the door. I looked suitably concerned and nodded away, willing them to be gone.

I waited only till I saw the tail-lights of the car disappear round the corner. Then I was out of the house and away on my bicycle, head down and pedalling like a mad thing towards the canal. I ran into traffic jams, but I managed to keep moving, weaving in and out of the cars, cutting across carparks. Then at long last I was clear of the traffic and bowling along under the prison walls, the canal running darkly across the other side of the road. I always hated going past the prison, especially in the evening. The whole place glowered at me, but it gave me an even greater incentive to pedal harder. I never stopped the whole way, not once.

From the lock gates I could see there was a light in Popsicle's boat. He was there, and as I cycled along the towpath past the barges, I was sure that he knew I was coming, that he would be waiting for me. I'd barely set foot on the gangplank when I heard him calling out to me.

'Cessie? Is that you? Come aboard. Come aboard.'

I found him down below in the glow of his cabin, lying on his bed, and grinning like the Cheshire cat. He was propped up on a pile of cushions, with his knees drawn up in front of him. His shoes were off and he wore no socks. He was wriggling his toes at me.

'Long walk. My feet are killing me.' He had a tin in his hand. I knew at once it had to be condensed milk. He held it up. 'Remember this, Cessie?' He swung his legs off the bed, stood up and came towards me. 'Well, what do you think of the old *Lucie Alice*? Isn't she the most beautiful thing you ever saw? And she's not just pretty either. Two forty-horsepower diesel engines. You can hardly hear yourself thinking when she's at full throttle. Eight and a half knots, two hundred miles without

refuelling, and – unlike yours – she's quite unsinkable.'
He was close to me now, his hands on my shoulders,
and his eyes were burning bright into mine.

'Thanks to you, Cessie, I know it all now. It's all here,
in this boat, all around me, and you found her for me,
Cessie. I got your school book. Harry said it was
important, and it was too.' I looked down and saw my
English book lying open beside the half-finished model
of the battleship. 'Lucie Alice . . . Dunkirk,' he went on.
'You gave it all back to me, Cessie; but this old tin helped
a bit, I'm sure of it. You can smile, but it was like Popeye
with his spinach. Like a flood it was, Cessie. The
moment I lay there on that bed and tasted it, all the
memories came flooding through me. I'm telling you,
Cessie, I was dizzy with it.'

He picked up another tin from the desk behind him.
'Here,' he said. 'I've got dozens more in the cupboard.
You can have a whole tin to yourself, if you like. You've
had it before, have you? You turned your nose up at it,
if I remember rightly. One taste and you won't put it
down. Guaranteed.' And he stabbed two holes in it
with his knife, settled me down in one of the big
armchairs in the middle of the cabin, and sat himself
down opposite me.

I had never tasted anything so sickly sweet, nor so

completely and overwhelmingly delicious.

'They'll be out looking for you, you know,' I said.

'Well, they won't find us here, will they? You haven't said anything, have you?' I shook my head, and sucked in another mouthful of condensed milk.

Then I asked the one question I'd been longing to ask him: 'Who's Lucie Alice, the girl in the photo?'

It was some time before he replied. 'Well, after all you've done for me, Cessie, if anyone's got a right to know, then you have. I'm warning you before I start, there's things I'm going to tell you you'll find hard to believe. But it'll all be true, true as I'm sitting here. You keep knocking back your condensed milk and I'll tell you the lot, beginning to end.'

He took a deep breath, and then he began.

'I don't rightly know where I was born, Cessie. Never knew who my mother was, nor my father. So that bit's easy. First thing I remember was the house in Lowestoft. Barnardo's home it was – fifteen, maybe twenty of us. And it was all right too. I wasn't miserable, nothing like that. If you don't have a proper family in the first place, then you can't miss them, can you? I'm afraid I was a bit of a tearaway as a young lad, always in trouble: bunking off school, scrumping for apples, and poaching too – rabbits, pheasants, trout – whatever I could find. Time and again I'd get myself caught, and of course I'd get a good wigging for my trouble. Didn't stop me. Never seemed to learn my lesson somehow.

'You could see the sea from my bedroom window, and I never wanted to be away from it. All I wanted to do when I grew up was go to sea. And do you know why? It wasn't just the beauty of it, nor the wildness of it. It wasn't the salt on your lips, or the shrieking of the gulls, not for me. It was the boats, and one boat in particular – the Lowestoft lifeboat. To watch that lifeboat shooting down the slipway and go plunging into the sea, to see her ploughing her way out into the waves – it's all I lived for. Nothing like it, nothing in all the world. Whenever she went out, all weathers, I'd be there, down on the beach waiting for them to come back. And afterwards, I'd follow the crew through the streets, as they walked up to the pub. I'd be outside the window listening to their talk. All I wanted as a lad was to be near them, to be like them, to be one of them.

'I was fifteen years old, big for my age and strong too. I was out there, along with half the town, when the new lifeboat was launched. Forty-six foot, Watson cabin-type, she was; bright yellow funnel, shining blue with a red stripe round the gunwales. I never saw anything so beautiful in all my life.

'Later that day, I was walking round her in the shed at the top of the slipway, stroking her from end to end, when I first saw her name: *Michael Hardy*. Now I don't know who gave me my name when I was little, but all my life I'd been called Michael, Michael Stevens. And here was this lifeboat with half my own name on her. Silly, maybe, but I knew then that it was a meant thing with me and the *Michael Hardy*, that we belonged together. One day I would be a lifeboatman in that boat. I would pull on the blue jersey and the yellow oilskins. I would climb up into that boat and go roaring down the slipway. I would go to sea in her and save lives. So I went right up to the coxswain – I can't remember his name now, a great big bearded fellow – I walked right up to him next day in the town and I asked him, point blank. He laughed, and shook his head. "You're far too young," he says. "Come back in a couple of years," he says. I'll tell you, Cessie, I went away and I cried like a baby.

'By now everyone was talking about the war they knew was coming, but all I could think about was how they wouldn't let me join the crew of the *Michael Hardy*. I mooched about the beach all that summer. Every time I saw the lifeboat go down the slipway it was just more salt in the wound.'

The boat creaked above our heads and Popsicle looked up and smiled. 'I swear she talks to me sometimes. She listens too. The things she's seen in her time. The things she's heard. You know about Dunkirk, d'you?'

'Not much,' I said.

'And why should you? Long time ago, all of it. Summer of 1940, and there was a right old mess going on over there in France. The German army was knocking all hell out of everyone. They pushed the whole jolly lot of us back to the sea at Dunkirk: British, French, Belgians, all sorts. There were 250,000 men on the beaches of Northern France that had to be fetched back home; the whole army, or what was left of it. It was all on the radio, in the papers too. Next thing I heard, the navy were in Lowestoft, looking for all the boats they could find to bring the boys back home off the beaches. They were going to take the *Michael Hardy* over to Dunkirk. Well, I wasn't going to miss out on that, was I?

'No one was looking for stowaways, so it was easy enough. I crept on board the night before and found myself a hiding-place in the locker right under the bow, just about where my bed is now. I was too cold to sleep, too excited. Next morning there was a lot of stamping about and shouting up on deck. Then we were thundering down the slipway. We hit the sea with a great crash – it fairly shook me up, I can tell you. I thought I had broken every bone in my body. I remember the engines were pounding, and I was sick, sick as a dog with all the pitching and rolling. And it was cold, Cessie, bitter cold down there, and dark too. Never been so cold in all my life. I couldn't feel my feet at all. But honest to God, I'd never been so happy. I was at sea at last, in a lifeboat, in the *Michael Hardy*.

'I can't be sure, but I think I was more than a day down there in that locker before they found me. And do you know how they found me? I sneezed. They found me because I sneezed. I was hauled up on deck to explain myself. The officer wasn't best pleased, I can tell you. But what could he do? We were in the middle of the English Channel and the weather was blowing up a gale. He could hardly have me chucked overboard, could he? So he just gave me a right rollicking and sent me down to the galley to brew up the tea.

'Pretty soon after that they were all far too busy to bother with me anyway. There were fighter planes, Stukas, Messerschmitts, all diving at us out of nowhere; and ahead of us were great plumes of black smoke along the coast as if the whole place was on fire. And the little ships. All shapes and sizes. Hundreds of them, all ferrying the soldiers from the beaches to the Navy ships standing offshore. We waited until nightfall and then we went in close, into the harbour – or what was left of it. The whole sky was red with fire.

'We heard the soldiers first, and then we saw them. Lines and lines of them waist high, shoulder high in the water, helmets askew, rifles held over their heads. They were shouting at us, and some of them were crying. First time I'd ever seen grown men cry. They were grabbing at the ropes and we were hauling them on board. And off we went packed to the gunwales. You couldn't move for soldiers.

'Awful terrible wounds they had, some of them; and they were sea-sick too. Poor blighters. It doesn't bear thinking about. Terrified they were, some of them. And I was too. We were all frightened. I mean you couldn't not be. You could see the sea on fire where a ship had gone down, and there were men in the water screaming, and the shells kept coming and coming; and you knew that sooner or later one of them had to hit you.

'We'd done a couple of trips to and from the beaches when it happened. I was sitting high up on the bow of the boat, a crowd of soldiers all round me, when I saw this shape come towards us out of the darkness. It took me a few seconds before I realised it was a boat, and a few more before I saw that it was coming straight for us. She rammed us amidships and I was knocked right over the side and into the cold of the sea. Down I went. I never thought I'd come up, but I did. I was kicking and screaming for all I was worth, but it didn't do me any good. I just sank again like a stone.'

'Couldn't you swim?' I asked.

'Still can't,' said Popsicle, shaking his head. 'Isn't that mad? I've spent all my silly life on boats, and I still can't swim. So, anyway, I thought I was going to drown for certain; but suddenly there were arms round me and lifting me, and at last I was breathing blessed air again. It was one of the soldiers. He still had his tin hat on too. I remember that. "Hang on," he says. And I did, for dear life. He swum me ashore and we staggered up the sand and into the dunes.

'Of course we didn't sleep a wink. We were wet through to the skin, and freezing. The shelling never stopped all night long. Not a night I'd care to live through again, I can tell you.

'He was a nice young fellow, the one who pulled me out. We got chatting, the two of us. He'd only been in the army a few months, he said, and he'd done nothing but retreat the whole time. I told him about how I'd stowed away on the *Michael Hardy*. "Well," he says, "you'd better find yourself a uniform, and be quick about it; because if we don't get off the beaches and the Germans catch us, then they'll think you're a spy and they'll shoot you for certain." Do you know what he did? He took off his battledress top and gave it to me, there and then. "Here," he says. "You'd best have this, just in case. About the same size, we are." And it was true, too. Him and me, like two peas in a pod. So I put it on.

'Five minutes later, that's all, and we were sitting there side by side shivering in the dunes, when the fighters came back, strafing and bombing all along the beach. Everyone was running for it; but there was nowhere to run to, I could see that. The soldier and me, we just stayed where we were and flattened ourselves in the sand. The ground shook, like an earthquake it was, and the sand showered down on us. I thought it would never stop. There was a horrible silence after that. Then I heard the crying and the moaning. I felt blood on my face, warm blood. I knew I'd been hit in the head. There wasn't much pain, but my head was spinning. I seemed to be floating, almost like I was in the sea, and it was getting darker all around me, darker than it should have been. I remember the soldier's eyes were open in the darkness. They were looking straight at me, but he wasn't seeing me. I knew he was dead. I knew then that I would soon be dead, just like he was. I was sure of it. I wasn't frightened any more. Funny that.

'I woke up and there were gulls flying overhead, screeching just like they did at home. I thought for a moment I was back home in Lowestoft. I really did. But not for long. I sat up and looked around me. The tide was up. There was no more shelling. It was quiet, like the quiet after a storm. The place was littered with trucks, jeeps, guns – some still burning – and there were bodies, everywhere bodies lying on the sand. One of the soldiers rolled over in the shallows, and he seemed for a moment to be alive. He wasn't. No one was, except me. The armada of little ships was gone, except for the wrecks left behind out at sea – or beached – and there were dozens of them, dozens. The soldier who had saved me was still looking at me. I had to get away.

'I got to my feet and climbed up over the dunes. No one was moving in the town. Everyone was dead, or everyone was gone – that's what it felt like anyway. I wandered up into the smoking ruins of the town, not knowing where I was going nor why. I suppose I was just looking for someone who was alive, anyone. My legs wouldn't work like they should and I kept reeling and stumbling up against the walls of the houses. Then they just gave way completely, and I found myself sitting down in the doorway of a house and I couldn't move any more. I heard a sort of rumbling and a rattling, and it was coming closer and getting louder all the time.

'Suddenly the door opened behind me and I was dragged in off the street. I found myself in a darkened room and there was this lady standing over me, her finger to her lips. She didn't want me to talk. So I didn't. She was peeping out through the closed shutters. I crawled over to have a look. Tanks, and there were soldiers behind them, German soldiers, hundreds of them.

'That poor woman, she had to drag me all the way up the stairs. I couldn't help myself much. By the time we got to the top I knew there were two of them, one had me by the legs, the other had her arms under my shoulders. They took me into a bedroom and I thought they'd put me on the bed, but they didn't. They put me in a clothes cupboard instead, a great big thing it was and it smelled of mothballs. They turned out to be mother and daughter, and they looked like it too. Same dark hair, pale skin. They were terrified, just like I was. But the young one, she gave me a smile, the sort of smile that said it was going to be all right. "Lucie Alice," she whispered, *"Je suis Lucie Alice."* Then she closed the cupboard door and I was left in the darkness lying at the bottom of that musty old cupboard, the clothes dangling all around my face.'

Popsicle's voice was faltering now as he went on. 'The things they did for me, those two. Patched me up, fed me, cared for me, just like I was their family. No one ever treated me like that before, not in my whole life. For days and days, they let me out only for five minutes at a time, to stretch my legs, go to the toilet – that sort of thing. I knew why, of course. I could hear the soldiers, plain enough, just outside, down in the street. I had to stay in the cupboard, and I wasn't ever to come out unless they said so. I did as I was told and stayed put, and it was just as well I did too. They came looking. One evening it was. I was half asleep in the bottom of my cupboard. I heard them coming up the stairs and into the room, stamping around in their boots. I curled myself up tight under the clothes, closed my eyes, and stopped breathing. They opened the cupboard door too, had a look, but they never moved the clothes, so they never found me. But if they had . . .

'You've got to remember, Cessie, that if they'd found me they'd have shot the two of them for sure. That's something, eh? They did that for me, and they didn't even know me. After the house had been searched that time, they reckoned it was safer. So they let me out of my cupboard a bit more often, and for longer too; but I still had to stay in my room and stay away from the window. I was never to open the shutters, Lucie Alice told me, never to look out of the window.

'Of course, I couldn't understand much of what they were saying, not to start with; but I got the gist of it all right. They were going to find a way to get me out and back home to England. But it would take time. I had to be patient. I didn't mind waiting, I can tell you. The more I saw of Lucie Alice, the less I wanted to go home anyway. She'd come to my room often, and not only to bring me my meals either. She did most of the talking, and every day I understood better and better what she was saying.

'We only had a month together, Cessie, but I loved that girl. I really loved her.' He picked up the photograph. 'She gave me this. "So you won't forget me," she said. See what she wrote on the back? "*Pour toujours.*" Means "For ever". And she meant it too, I know she did.' He turned the photograph over in his hand. 'Great brown eyes she had, Cessie, and her hair . . . I never touched anyone else's hair before hers. Soft as air.' It was a moment or two before he was able to go on.

'She kept warning me and warning me to stay in the cupboard, just in case. But I hated it in that cupboard, Cessie. I couldn't stand being shut up; and, besides, I couldn't read my book in there. I had this book of poems called *The Golden Treasury*. I'd found it in the pocket of that soldier's battledress. Bit wrinkled with the damp it was, but you could read it, just about. First time I'd ever read any poems. Wonderful they were. Wonderful. So anyway, from time to time, I'd come out of my cupboard and read my poems. I'd read them out loud too, and learn them off by heart. One morning I was on my own in the house and I'd been reading a few of my poems. Maybe I was feeling a bit restless. I don't know. But I did what Lucie Alice always told me not to do – I went to the window. I thought it was safe enough. I couldn't see anyone down in the street, so I opened the shutter just a little and peeked out.

'I hadn't noticed the soldier. He was standing just across the street from me, under the lamppost, and he was smoking. He was blowing smoke rings in the air and watching them float away up towards me. Our eyes met just for a moment, but that was all it took. Before I even reached my cupboard I heard the street door crash open and boots pounding up the stairs. I had the cupboard door almost closed, but I was too late. He wrenched it out of my hand and there I was crouching in amongst the clothes, and he was smiling down at me like a cat that's got a mouse. Then there were other soldiers in the room. They hauled me out and I was marched off down the street with my hands in the air, a rifle jabbing into my back. We'd just turned the corner into the wide road along the seafront, when I saw Lucie Alice coming towards us on the same pavement, a loaf of bread under her arm. We both knew there mustn't be a flicker of recognition between us. That was the last I ever saw of her.

'I always kept her photo in my book of poems. When they searched me they found the book, of course, and the photo of Lucie Alice inside, but they never took much notice of it. They must've thought it was my girl back home. They let me keep my book of poems and the photo too.

'I spent a few uncomfortable nights in a prison cell, with a few other soldiers they'd rounded up. They questioned me over and over again about the people who had hidden me, but I just played dumb and shrugged my way through it. I kept saying I didn't know who they were, nor anything about them. In the end, I think they believed me. "We'll find them anyway. We know their names. They can't run for ever," said the officer. "And when we do, we'll put them up against a wall and shoot them." Then he wished me a happy war in my prison camp and packed me off with the others in a lorry to Germany.'

I was so wrapped up in his story that I had quite forgotten my condensed milk. I remembered now. I sucked in another mouthful and waited for him to begin again.

'Prison camp was all boredom, cabbagey old soup, black bread and boredom. And the winters were cold, Cessie, so cold you couldn't sleep. Still, I had my *Golden Treasury* and my photo of Lucie Alice. That was something. Worst of all was not knowing all that time about what had happened to Lucie Alice and her mother. I wanted to write to them, but I couldn't, could I? I didn't want to give them away. They'd read your letters, everything you wrote. There were so many things I hated about that place: the locked doors at night, the searchlights, and the dogs and the wire all around us; and always these little Hitlers bawling at us, telling us what to do, what not to do. I'd look at the birds, Cessie. I'd watch them take off and fly out over the wire, go wherever they wanted. And I'd look out of the window of my hut sometimes, and I'd think those are the same stars they're looking at back in Lowestoft, the same stars Lucie Alice is looking at, if she's still alive. I never stopped thinking about her.

'I taught myself French. It was hard at first, but I had a pal in the camp who knew a bit of French, and he gave me a hand. We got hold of all the French books we could – you can learn an awful lot in five years if you haven't got much else to do. And I wanted to learn because I wanted to be able to talk her language when I got out, when the war was over.

'The best thing of all though wasn't the French lessons, it was the Red Cross parcels. It was like Christmas every time they came.' He held up his tin of condensed milk. 'That's when I first tasted this – out of a Red Cross parcel in the camp.

'Those five years behind the wire were like a lifetime. Then one morning we woke up and the guards were gone. The gates were open and there were American soldiers marching down the road towards the camp! It was all over and done with. I was twenty-one years old and there was only one thing I was sure about – I was never ever going to allow myself to be shut up again. The war ended soon after and I was sent back home to England.

'I wrote to Lucie Alice, telling what had happened, asking how she was, thanking her and her mother for all they'd done for me. I told her I still loved her and I always would. I even asked her to marry me. But she never wrote back. I wrote again and again. No reply. Then one of the letters was sent back. "Not known", it said on the envelope. After that, I'll be honest with you, I tried to put her out of my mind. If she was dead, it had been my fault. Then I met your grandmother, and things took another turn.

'I'd found a job boatbuilding in Hull, and I was delivering a fishing boat from Hull down to Bradwell. I liked the place, liked the people. There was a job in a small boatyard, and so I stayed. Then one evening I bumped into Cecilia down on the quay. She was looking at the sunset and I was looking at her. Pretty as a picture, she was. Six months later we were married. We found a place to live, and then little Arthur comes along. The boatbuilding business wasn't going that well. I did a bit of fishing too on the side to make ends meet. Things weren't easy, but we were doing all right, I thought, making a living of sorts.'

For a few moments Popsicle said nothing more. I thought he'd finished, but then he went on. 'The truth is, Cessie, I should never have done what I did. I should never have got married. Sometimes I think I only did it to make myself forget Lucie Alice, and that wasn't fair on your grandmother. We were never suited. She knew it. I knew it. We were just making each other more and more miserable every day. I was off drinking in the Green Man, drowning my sorrows, and she began to hate me for not loving her like I should have. I don't blame her. Then she met this other fellow, this Bill; and off she went, her and Bill and little Arthur, and that's the last I saw of them. Not exactly a happy-ever-after story, is it?'

'Not exactly,' I said. 'What about the lifeboat? You must've found it again somehow.'

'I was coming to that. After Cecilia left, and little Arthur, I never lived in a proper house again, not till I come to live with you anyway. I picked up work here and there in boatyards all over the country, and I made decent money too. But I always lived on a boat, always on the water. I moved around, became a bit of a water gypsy, I suppose. I went where the work was, wherever I felt like going. Then, maybe ten years ago, I came across this old lifeboat rotting away in a boatyard in Poole. You guessed it, it was the *Michael Hardy*. Pure luck. I'd saved a bit, over the years – nothing much to spend it on, I suppose. She was going for a song, and so I bought her. It took me five years to put her to rights, back to what she was. I only changed one thing, her name. I called her *Lucie Alice*. I don't have to tell you why, do I?'

I needed to ask something else and now seemed the right moment.

'But I still don't understand, Popsicle. Why didn't you go back to France and look for her, for Lucie Alice?'

He sighed, and then smiled sadly. 'I've been asking myself that same question, just about every day of my life, I should think. Up to now it's always been the same answer, and it's not easy to explain, Cessie. But I'll try. It's like this. Whilst I don't know what happened to her, I've got hope, some little hope that she's still alive somewhere. The chances are of course that she's been dead all these years, I know that; but if I don't know that for certain, then at least I can think of her as if she's still alive, can't I? Once I'd found out that she was dead, then it'd be the end of all my hope, wouldn't it? And let's say I did find her and she was alive after all, what would she think of me, I mean after what I'd done? I'd betrayed her, hadn't I? Her and her mother. I looked out of that window when I shouldn't have. So I'd lose both ways, wouldn't I? That's what I thought, until . . . until now that is.'

'What d'you mean?'

'Well, I was sitting here thinking, just before you

came. That little stroke I had – it was a warning, that's how I see it. It was telling me something, telling me that for better or worse, and before it's too late, I'd better go and look for Lucie Alice and find out what really did happen all those years ago. And then maybe, just maybe, I can put things right between us. I've been running away from this all my life, Cessie. Not any more. Not any more. I even know the street where she lived. It's in the photo. You've got to look carefully, but it's there.'

He showed me the photo again and, sure enough, I could just make out the street name above Lucie Alice's head: *Rue de la Paix*.

'It's not far,' Popsicle went on. 'And you never know, Cessie, I could get lucky. Maybe I'll find her. Maybe she'll still be there.'

The idea came into my head at once and I didn't hesitate. 'Can I come? Please, Popsicle, I can help. Honest I can. You'll need someone to help, won't you? I can do the mooring ropes. I can be on look-out. I can cook. Anything. Please?'

He was looking at me long and thoughtfully. 'You and me, Cessie, we think like one person sometimes, I swear we do. I was just wondering how I was going to manage the old girl all the way over to Dunkirk on my own.' He reached forward suddenly and took my hand. 'Would you do it?' he asked. 'Would you really come with me?'

'When?' I said. 'When do we go?'

'Soon as I've fixed a few things up,' he said. 'Soon as the tide's right.'

11 THE GREAT ESCAPE

AN HOUR LATER POPSICLE WAS STILL BENDING over his charts. There were tins of condensed milk all around to hold the edges down. He'd done his calcula-tions in complete silence, his brow furrowed in deep concentration.

'Almost there, Cessie,' he said at last, reaching across the table for a slim grey booklet. 'Tides,' he went on, as he searched for the right page. 'Mariner's bible, this is. You've got to know the time of the tides, high tide, low tide. You can't move unless you know that. It should be just about right Saturday next, that's what I'm hoping. One thing you've always got to remember about the sea, Cessie, is that you can only do what she'll let you do.' He found what he was looking for. 'I thought so. I thought so. Full moon Saturday night. High tide just after midnight. Perfect. Could be cloud cover, of course, but that doesn't matter. We'll have enough light to see our way out of here. We don't want it blowing a gale of course. Keep our fingers crossed, eh? With a bit of luck we'll make it in five or six hours. It's sixty-three miles to Dunkirk, less than I thought. We should be there before first light. We'll come in in the dark. Better that way. If they don't see us, then there won't be any questions, will there? And if they do see us, well then, we'll just have to talk our way out of trouble, won't we? Done it before.' He closed the book. 'So, you'll need to be here by midnight next Saturday. Are you sure you can make it?'

'Sure,' I said. But I wasn't at all sure of any of it. I only knew that I wanted to go with him. Of that I was quite sure.

'Good girl. But there's one thing you've got to do for me, and I don't want you forgetting it. I want you to leave a note for your mum and your dad. We don't want them worrying themselves to death, do we? Just tell them that you've gone off with me for a couple of days, that I'll bring you back home again soon. And whilst you're at it, tell them goodbye from me. Tell them no hard feelings. Time for me to move on, that's all.'

'What d'you mean?' I asked.

'I told you, Cessie. I can't abide being shut in – cupboards, prison camps, Shangri-La – all the same to me. I don't ever want to go back. Don't get me wrong. It's not a bad place, except for that Dragonwoman. I've got good friends up there, and I'll miss them. But it's not for me, not in a million years. No, Cessie, this is my home, this boat. Whatever happens over there in Dunkirk, whether I go barmy or not, here's where I'll end my days, on my own boat, with the sky above me and the sea all around me. It's where I belong.'

I pleaded with him even though I knew it was useless. 'But I'll tell them. I'll tell Mum and Dad what's happened, that you've remembered everything, and you're better, completely better. You'll be able to come home. They won't send you back to Shangri-La. I know they won't. I won't let them.'

He was shaking his head as I was talking. 'No, Cessie, don't you go telling them anything of the kind, anything at all come to that. And don't you go blaming them for sending me up to Shangri-La. The way I was carrying on, they had no choice. I was a liability. That's what I was, a liability. I've caused them enough trouble, enough pain.'

'But you're better,' I insisted, quite unable now to hold back my tears.

'Yes, I'm better, better than I've ever been, thanks to you – and now I'm going to do just what I should've done all those years ago. I'm going to go over there and find out what happened to Lucie Alice, and I don't want anyone trying to stop me. So we'll keep everything just between the two of us. No one else must know a thing. Promise me, Cessie.'

'Promise,' I said.

He reached forward and wiped my face with his sleeve. 'And no more tears either, Cessie. I can't cope at all if you do that.' I did what I could to sniff them back. 'That's better,' he said. 'Now, I'll get myself back to Shangri-La, and you'd best get off home quick. They'll be getting anxious, and we don't want that. I've got a thing or two to finish off here, before I go – check the batteries, see if I've got enough diesel in the tanks, that sort of thing. We don't want the engines packing up on us in mid-channel, do we? Not with all those giant tankers steaming up and down.'

He took me up on deck and walked with me as far as the gangplank. 'Saturday midnight,' he said. 'Don't be late.' I looked up into his face. It was ghostly white against the dark of the night sky. The thought came over me that Popsicle might not be real at all, that he was a mere figment of my imagination, that maybe I was living all this only inside a dream. I needed to reassure myself. I stood on tiptoe and threw my arms round his neck. He was real enough. I was down on the towpath before he spoke again.

'Oh and, Cessie, bring lots of warm clothes, there's a girl. You'll need them. And that fiddle of yours too. Nothing like the sound of music out at sea. It'll keep our spirits up.'

There was plenty of music to face when I got back home. I was hardly in through the front door before it began. I didn't argue, but I did defend myself.

'I just went looking for him, that's all. What's so wrong with that?' Then I remembered to ask: 'Haven't they found him yet?'

'Not yet,' said my mother. I could see that she had been crying. 'But they will,' she went on. 'They will find him, won't they, Arthur?' She turned away from me and buried her head in my father's shoulder. It was only then that I realised how much they were suffering, my father as much as my mother. I had a sudden longing to comfort them, to tell them everything I knew, everything that had happened to me that night. But I could not bring myself to do it. Popsicle had confided in me. I'd given him my promise.

'I bet,' I said, inventing as I went along, 'I bet he's

just gone off for a wander or something. He'll find his way back sooner or later, you'll see.' It was the best I could do without giving anything away.

Later I made them a cup of tea – not something I often did – and brought it into the sitting-room. They were sitting side by side on the sofa and holding hands. Their faces lit up when they saw me come in with the tray, and I liked that. 'Popsicle can take care of himself,' I said, pouring the tea. 'He's a survivor, Dad; you said it yourself. Wherever he is, he'll be all right. I know he will.'

As we sat there waiting, I was trying to think of more reassuring things to say, but I knew I had to be careful. I had to be seen to be anxious too. So I kept silent. It was the safest way.

Suddenly my father was on his feet and standing with his back to the fireplace, his hands thrust deep in his pockets. 'I'm going to say something, something that's got to be said.' He looked uncertain as to whether he should go on. 'You're going to hate me for this,' he said, catching my eye.

'What? What is it?' my mother was on the edge of the sofa.

'All right, all right.' He still didn't want to let it out. 'All along, ever since he came here, I haven't been fair to him. I know that, and I'm not proud of it either. The truth is, I think I may have sent him up to Shangri-La, not just for his own good, but partly to hurt him, like he hurt me when I was a kid. I think I really wanted him to sit up there and long for us to come and visit, just so he'd know what it was like.' His whole face was overwhelmed with tears now. 'Day after day, year after year, I'd be sitting up on that wall outside the home, and I'd be looking down the road, believing he'd come round the corner and take me away, and he never did. I've always hated him for that, always. I know I shouldn't have, but I did.'

'But you're not like that,' my mother whispered. 'That's spiteful, vengeful.'

'Yes, all of that,' my father went on, 'and worse, too. He could be lying out there under a bus right now, or mugged in some dark alleyway; and if he is, it'll be like I killed him myself, my own father.' He was reaching out for understanding, for comfort, and I didn't know how to give it. 'I should've been like you, like both of you. I should've welcomed him and with open arms, but I couldn't. I should have forgiven him by now. I'm a grown man, for Christ's sake. I should have had it in me to . . .'

The telephone rang. My mother was there first. We

followed her into the front hall. She wasn't doing much of the talking. All she said was: 'Yes . . . Yes . . . thank you.' Then she put the phone down and turned to us. She was beaming through her tears. 'He's all right. Popsicle's all right. It seems he just walked up to a policeman in town and said he'd like a lift up to Shangri-La. He's fine. He's safe.'

The hug that followed was a threesome one, and lasted and lasted. 'We'll bring him home,' said my father when it was over. 'We'll bring him home.'

The week that followed seemed more like a month. Every night, every day I spent thinking of Popsicle, of Saturday, of Dunkirk, of Lucie Alice. At school Shirley Watson plied me with endless questions about the *Lucie Alice*, questions I fended off as best I could without offending her. I told her as much of the truth as I dared – it always helps when you're telling a lie. I explained that Popsicle loved lifeboats because he'd worked on one long ago, when he was a young man. He must've seen the *Lucie Alice* down on the canal, and used her as a model for my boat. She believed me, I thought, but I wasn't quite sure. I couldn't be sure of anything with Shirley Watson. Certainly, she seemed to have become an ally, a friend even; a turn-around I welcomed but still could not quite trust.

At home hurried preparations were under way to have Popsicle home again. My father was arranging for a nurse to come in to be with him each weekday until he was well enough to be on his own. But the nurse couldn't come until after the weekend. We'd surprise Popsicle, he said. We'd go up there on Sunday and we'd just tell him out of the blue that he was coming home. We'd pick up his things there and then and bring him home with us.

They were so much looking forward to it all; but of course, all the time they were planning I knew it was never going to happen, that by Sunday, Popsicle and I would be gone to France, they'd have found my letter – the letter I was still trying to compose – and they'd know the worst. So many times I nearly told them. I longed to unburden myself of my secret, but I could not and I would not betray Popsicle. I held my secret inside me and willed the days to pass.

I didn't finish my letter until the Saturday morning. I'd tried to write it all out, to explain everything, to tell Popsicle's whole life story; but when I read it through it seemed so unlikely, as if I'd concocted the whole thing. Maybe it was the way I'd written it. I wrote pages and pages, but it all ended up in the wastepaper basket. In the end I settled for the briefest of notes:

Dear Mum and Dad,

Please don't worry about me. I've gone off with Popsicle for a couple of days. There's something he's got to do and he needs me to help him. That's why I'm not here. Don't worry. I'll be quite safe and I'll be home soon.

Love from

Cessie.

We spent the Saturday afternoon making 'Welcome Home Popsicle' signs, one for the front door, one for his bedroom door. We brought out the box of Christmas decorations from under the stairs, and festooned the sitting-room with streamers and balloons. We hung the Christmas tree lights over the mantelpiece. I blew up so many balloons that my head ached with it.

In spite of the deception I was playing out, it was a lovely time, because the three of us were together, really together as we hadn't been for a long time. My father never once talked of going to work, nor even answered the phone. And my mother hardly mentioned 'her' school or 'her' children. I wished it could always be like this.

I hoped they'd get off to bed early, and I tried to encourage them to do so by going up to have my bath straight after supper.

'See you in the morning,' said my father. I think it took him by surprise when I kissed him goodnight. I hadn't done that for weeks. 'Tomorrow's the great day then,' he said, holding on to my hand for a moment longer.

'Yes, Dad,' I said, hating myself for what I was about to do to them.

'Don't run all the hot water off,' my mother called after me. 'I'll come up and see you. Won't be long.'

When she did come up an hour or so later, she found me in bed seemingly asleep with my light turned out. Over the chair my clothes were all ready to step into, and behind the chair two extra jumpers, and my anorak. My violin was under the bed – I hadn't forgotten it.

'Asleep?' she whispered. I didn't reply because, in my state of high excitement, I couldn't trust my voice not to give me away. She closed the door quietly. I lay there in the darkness, riven with guilt. I knew well enough how much anguish I was about to cause, but I could see no other way I could fulfil my promise to Popsicle.

I tried not to shut my eyes. I had to stay awake. The last thing I wanted to do was to fall asleep and not wake up in time. I just wished they'd turn off the television and come up to bed. But they didn't. The television hummed and burbled downstairs, lulling me out of my resolve.

Only when I woke did I realise I'd been asleep. I sat up with a jolt. My bedside clock said eleven fifteen. The house was dark and quiet all around me. I knew where everything was without turning on the light. I was dressed, down the stairs, and out of the front door within a couple of minutes. With my violin clipped to the rack behind me, I cycled out of the estate and into town as fast as I could go. The roads were practically empty. I heard midnight strike from the church as I cycled over the canal bridge. I'd made it, just.

I could see the barges quite clearly in the moonlight, and beyond them the wider hull of the *Lucie Alice*. But there were no lights on board. She was as dark as the barge next to her. There was no one there. As I wheeled my bike along the towpath, I began to think, and worry and doubt. Perhaps Popsicle wasn't that much better after all. Perhaps he still had bouts of forgetfulness. Perhaps he was barmy. Or maybe the whole story about Lucie Alice, about Dunkirk, was some kind of old man's fantasy. Perhaps Popsicle was lying fast asleep in his bed up at Shangri-La, our rendezvous quite forgotten.

I left my bike lying in the undergrowth beside the towpath, and went on board. I called out for him as loudly as I dared. The moon slipped behind a cloud and the world darkened suddenly. A warm shiver of fear crept up the back of my neck. I went below. The cabin door was still locked. I felt for and found the key in the tea tin. Popsicle was definitely not there. I thought then that maybe he'd said Sunday night, not Saturday night. I went up on deck. The moon was out again and gave me new hope. It was as round, as perfectly full, as it could possibly be. Full moon was Saturday, Popsicle had said so. It had to be tonight, midnight tonight.

There was the sound of an approaching car, head-lights sweeping out over the canal, briefly illuminating the entire length of the *Lucie Alice*, and blinding me as they did so. I ducked down below the gunwales. I could hear the car bumping along the towpath towards me. It stopped. The engine died and there was silence again. I had to look. It wasn't a car. It was a minibus, a white minibus with writing on the side. One of the words was definitely 'Shangri-La'. Popsicle was getting out of the driver's side and coming round the front of the minibus. He smiled up at me.

'Bit late, Cessie. Beggar wouldn't start,' he said.

The nearside door opened and the side doors slid back. I counted them as they got out. I could not believe what I was seeing. Twelve. I recognised Harry as one of them. He wasn't in his wheelchair. He was walking, bent between two sticks. There was an old lady beside him, helping him along. 'You know Harry, don't you?' said Popsicle, 'and this is Mary. Used to be a nurse, did Mary. She's seeing to all the medicines for us, aren't you, Mary?' He clapped his hands. 'Everyone, everyone. This is my granddaughter, this is the Cessie I've been telling you all about.'

They were all coming on board and they all seemed to know exactly where to go as well.

Popsicle was beside me, his arm round my shoulder. He was showing me off. Some of them ruffled my hair as they passed; one of the old ladies – later I found out that everyone called her 'Big Bethany' – touched my cheek with her cold hand and said, 'Just like you said, Popsicle, a princess. That's what we'll call her then, Princessie.' And they all laughed at that.

'Ancient mariners we may be,' Popsicle told me proudly. 'But we'll do fine. We've got blankets, food, water, all we need.'

I watched Harry's wheelchair being carried on board and the gangplank hauled in. 'Don't worry, Cessie. We did a dummy run, two nights ago. "Borrowed" the minibus for a couple of hours,' Popsicle went on. 'I showed them what was what. Everyone's got a job to do. They all know what they're doing.'

I could only stand and watch and admire as they bustled purposefully about the boat.

'Do they know everything? About Lucie Alice?' I asked.

'Everything,' Popsicle replied. 'The whole thing, beginning to end. I reckoned we were going to need all the help we could get. They volunteered, Cessie, to a man, to a woman. Of course there's some that couldn't make it; not well enough. But those we've got are raring to go. Isn't that right, Harry?'

'Only one thing I'm going to miss,' said Harry, 'and that's the Dragonwoman's face in the morning when she finds out that half her inmates have done a bunk!' Harry had settled himself down in his wheelchair and Mary was wrapping his legs in a blanket. 'Some ship, eh Cessie?' he said.

Some ship, some crew, I was thinking. All about me the ancient mariners went about making the lifeboat ready for sea. The lights came on down below, tarpaulins were rolled and stowed away. Popsicle was everywhere it seemed, helping, reminding, cajoling. There was no doubt who the skipper was. Everyone had a part to play – except me, it seemed. I was beginning to feel a bit redundant, until Popsicle took me to one side.

'Soon as I start up the engines, Cessie,' he said, 'I

want you to go and tell Sam up at the lock-keeper's house that we're ready. You know him already, don't you? He told me all about your little meeting. He'll be expecting you. Give him a hand with the lock gates, will you? Then, once we're through, I want you back on board and for'ard, keeping your eyes peeled for buoys and ropes and what have you. We won't get to Dunkirk with a rope wrapped round our propellers, will we?'

As the engines roared to life, I dashed along the towpath, over the canal bridge and hammered on Sam's door. He must have been ready and waiting, because the door opened almost at once, and he was standing there in his wellies and his dressing-gown, a torch in his hand. He looked at the *Lucie Alice*, all lit up like a Christmas cake from bow to stern, her ancient crew hauling in the lines, Popsicle at the wheel, with Harry beside him in his wheelchair.

'I need pinching,' said Sam. He never stopped chortling the whole time as we opened the lock gate and let in the *Lucie Alice*. The wheel was heavy and stiff, and there was a lot of huffing and puffing before the gate was fully open. She inched into the lock, engines chuntering sonorously. It was a very tight fit. We closed the gates behind her. As the lock flooded, she rose majestically up towards us. Only now that she was away from the barges and on her own, did I see just how magnificent she really was. Sam spoke my thoughts. 'Never seen anything like it,' he said. 'I just hope Popsicle knows what he's doing, that's all. It's an awful long way over to Dunkirk. Still, you've got the weather. Should be like a millpond out there tonight.'

As the deck of the *Lucie Alice* reached ground level, Popsicle was there to help me jump back on board. 'You see anything for'ard, Cessie, you let me know – loud,' he said. I made my way to the bow, stood on tiptoe, hooked my elbows over and looked down into the black of the water.

Minutes later we were out of the lock. The engines throttled up and we moved slowly into the harbour itself. The sea was bright with the moon and clear ahead as far as I could see. Below me the bow of the *Lucie Alice* was cutting her way through the water, and I felt the first salt spray on my face. I licked the salt off my lips, and breathed in deep.

As we steamed out across the harbour. I could see the silhouettes of fishing boats by the quay, and the cranes standing guard over them like skeletal sentinels. The lighthouse at the end of the harbour wall was closer now and flashing brighter all the time. Then we were underneath it and the swell of the open sea took us and rocked us. Sam had been wrong. It was no millpond out there. I heard laughter behind me as we crashed into our first significant wave – nervous laughter it was. The old lifeboat groaned and shuddered and ploughed on.

The cold of the spray took my breath away. Above me the moon rode the clouds, at just the same speed as the *Lucie Alice* rode the sea. She would be keeping up with us all the way, I thought. Out ahead of me, the sea glistened and glowed, and I knew that beyond the dark horizon lay Dunkirk and France. I thought of the last time she had made this trip all those years ago to pick up the soldiers off the beaches. I just hoped and prayed (and I really did pray) that Lucie Alice would be there in Dunkirk, just as she had been then.

Once we were well out to sea, I made my way back to Popsicle at the wheel. Harry's chair was being lashed down and Mary was wrapping him in another blanket, all the time urging him to come below with the others. But Harry would have none of it. 'I'm not going to miss this, Mary, not in a million years. So you can stop your fussing, I'm staying put.'

Popsicle enveloped me in his coat and let me take the wheel with him. 'We're on our way then,' he said. 'You did leave a note for your mum and dad, like I told you?'

'Yes.'

'That's good. Keep her steady now. Can you feel her, Cessie? Can you feel the heart of her?' I could too. 'Excited, isn't she? I reckon she knows exactly where she's going. Back to Dunkirk. And, please God, let it be back to Lucie Alice too.'

12 EARLIE IN THE MORNING

IT WAS AS IF I WAS SETTING OFF ON SOME GREAT and grand adventure, some wonderful quest, with a bunch of silverhaired Argonauts, and with Popsicle at the helm as our Jason. But these Argonauts around me were not strapping, muscle-bound Greek heroes. They were a dozen very old-age pensioners whose combined age, I worked out, must have totalled nearly a thousand years.

From their incessant jovial banter and the warmth of their camaraderie it would have been easy to believe that they were all on some Sunday outing; but Popsicle only had to say the word and they at once became a crew, slow about the boat maybe, but serious and purposeful. There were always four up on deck on watch, two for'ard, two aft, and Popsicle himself never left the wheel. We did hour-long shifts, and when we went below there was always a mug of hot sweet tea waiting, jam sandwiches for some, baked beans on toast for others.

I never did get to know all of them – there were too many for that – and besides no one really introduced me. They all treated me as if they knew me already, and I liked that. I got to know Benny though because he told me all about himself. The galley was Benny's domain – he made that quite clear. Benny liked talking, he liked talking loudly and repeated himself often. Everyone shouted at him, and at first I wondered why. It wasn't long before I discovered that he was almost completely deaf. He'd been a chef in a hotel in Bournemouth for most of his working life, he said, and he'd never allowed hangers-on in his kitchen. So I could come into his galley only if I lent a hand. I found myself doing everything from washing up, to stirring beans, to spreading butter, to cutting crusts off bread.

'You got to give the customers what they want,' he explained, waving a wooden spoon at me for emphasis. 'I said, you got to give the customers what they want. Most of us can't be doing with crusts, not any more. Not any more. You know something, Princessie? You might not believe this, but I had 'em all out for my twenty-first birthday, the whole lot of them.' He wasn't always easy to understand. 'I said, the whole lot of them. Present from my mum, bless her heart. Have your teeth out, she says, and you won't have no trouble with them later on. And she was right too. I said, she was right too. Not many of us up at Shangri-La still got our teeth left. You take Chalky, he's like me. Not a tooth of his own left in his head, not one.'

Chalky, as everyone called him, scarcely ever left the engines. He'd grin toothlessly at me and wave an oily rag whenever he saw me. 'Loves engines, does Chalky – knows 'em inside out. Train driver in his time. Easygoing sort, wouldn't hurt a fly,' Benny told me, and then in a more confidential tone: 'But you watch out for Mac. Different kettle of fish altogether. Used to be a Sergeant Major in the Guards. Stickler for everything. I said, he's a stickler for everything. Everything got to be just so or he's not happy, not happy at all. And when he's not happy . . . You've got to watch out for Mac. I'm saying, you've got to watch out for Mac.'

I knew Mac already – Harry had pointed him out. He was the dapper one with the natty moustache, the only one of them who never seemed to smile at me. He patrolled the deck constantly, making sure we were all properly secured on our lifelines whenever we were up on deck. He kept checking Harry's chair was properly lashed down. He was there too whenever the watch changed, making sure no one slipped or stumbled as they came out on deck. Benny told me he had a glass eye, but I never did find out which it was.

Then there were the twin brothers, still identical at eighty-four, and known to everyone as Tweedledum and Tweedledee – both of them unsteady on their legs, and both of them always insisting on taking their turn on watch together. Benny told me all about them: 'Tweedledum and Tweedledee, they've been up at Shangri-La near enough fifteen years now – oldest inmates. Hardly been out of the place in all that time. Never been in a boat before, neither of them. Never been nowhere much. Kept an ironmongers shop all their lives up in Bradford. Never done nothing like this. Well, nor have any of us, come to that, except Popsicle of course. Those beans'll be sticking if you don't stir them, Princessie. I said, those beans'll be sticking if you don't stir them.'

It was hot and stifling down below. I don't know if it was the oily smell of the engines, or the bubbling beans in the galley, or just the roll of the boat, but whatever it was I began to feel queasy. I went up on deck to breathe in the fresh air and felt better at once. Popsicle called me over to him. He patted the wheel. 'Isn't she the best? Isn't she something? More than fifty years old and she still purrs like a kitten.' It sounded more like a roaring lion to me, but I didn't argue.

Harry handed me his empty tea mug to take back down to the galley. 'I'll tell you something, girl,' he said, 'I've never been so cold in all my life, and I've never had so much fun either. A real live adventure, isn't it? Even if your grandad has got us all here under false pretences, even if that whole story of his about Dunkirk and Lucie Alice is just a load of old cobblers, if it's one great big porky pie, I won't mind. None of us would. We're having the time of our lives, all of us. Being out here, like this, it makes a fellow feel alive again.'

'But it's not a story,' I protested. 'It's true . . .'

'Of course it is,' Harry said. 'I know that. And d'you know how I know? Because it's too fantastical, that's why. He couldn't make up a story like that even if he wanted to. Mind you, I had my doubts to start with – we all of us did. But once he'd brought us down to see the *Lucie Alice* a couple of nights back, we were well and truly hooked. And now here we are, out in the middle of the ocean with nothing but water all around us. Like a dream it is, like the best dream I ever had.'

'Never mind about the dreaming, Harry,' said

Popsicle. 'Just you keep your watch. We'll be getting out to mid-Channel soon and there's bigger ships than us out here, a lot bigger; and I want to see 'em coming in plenty of time. So you keep your eyes skinned, Harry, you hear me?'

'Aye, aye, skip,' said Harry, and he dragged his hand out from under his blanket and gave a mock salute.

It wasn't long after that that Mary and Harry had a real set-to. It all began when she said he'd catch his death if he stayed up on deck much longer. He told her it was his death and he'd catch it if he wanted to. Popsicle had to intervene and send him down below to the warmth of the cabin. 'You can always come up again later, Harry,' he said. Harry muttered something un-repeatable, and gave in gracelessly. Between them, Mac and Mary got him down the gangway, Harry grumbling all the way.

'You fetch that fiddle of yours, Cessie,' said Popsicle. 'It'll cheer him up, cheer us all up.'

So I sat in Harry's wheelchair and began to play. 'Yesterday', 'Michelle', 'When I'm Sixty-Four' – I played all the tunes I could remember. Popsicle sang along, and after each one they clapped, from all around me on the deck, from down below in the cabin. Even Chalky left his engines for a while and came up to listen. After

'Nowhere Man' – we'd done it really well, the best we'd ever done it – they even called for an encore. Big Bethany then suggested I should play something on my own. I did the *Largo* because I knew I wouldn't make any mistakes. The sound of the violin seemed thin and reedy to me. Much of it was smothered by the pulsating throb of the engine, any resonance whipped away and lost at once over the vastness of the sea; but they seemed to like it.

'Lovely,' said Big Bethany quietly. 'Lovely that was.' She *was* big too, big smile, big everything. I liked her the best of all of them, I think. My fingers were aching with the cold now. I put the violin down on my knees and blew into my hands. I thought I'd finished.

'Princessie?' It was Harry's voice from down below. 'How about "Sailing"? Do you know "Sailing"?' So we did 'Sailing' again and again and again. Everyone seemed to know it – better than I did. Then, over the pounding of the engine, Benny shouted up that he wanted 'What shall we do with the drunken sailor?' I couldn't feel my fingers by now, I was playing so far out of tune that it was almost unrecognisable, but they didn't seem to mind. We ended the very last chorus with a thunderous 'Earlie in the morning', and then, to my great relief, Popsicle brought the sing-song to an end. He called up the new watch and sent the rest of us below to get some sleep. No one argued, least of all me. I was exhausted by now, frozen through and longing for the warmth of the cabin, however smelly, however stifling. I went down and lay on Popsicle's bed. Big Bethany came and covered me with an eiderdown. She said she'd never in her life heard a violin played so sweetly. Until then I never knew that words could really warm you physically, but hers did. I curled myself into myself and fell asleep almost at once.

A bell was ringing in my ears as I woke. Then I discovered it wasn't in my ears at all. It was ringing somewhere above my head. I looked around me. There was no one with me in the cabin, no one at all. The engines were turning over gently and I could feel that the boat was barely moving through the water. I swung my legs off the bed and ran out of the cabin. I saw Chalky bending over his engines.

'Anything wrong?' I asked.

'Fog,' he said, without looking up. 'Lousy fog.'

Moments later I was up on deck and it was swirling all around me. The bell was sounding again somewhere forward. I couldn't see the bow of the boat at all. Popsicle was at the wheel. Everyone else, including Harry, was on watch all around the boat, like dark statues, each of them wrapped in a cocoon of their own fog. None of them moved. None of them spoke. Popsicle saw me.

'We're listening,' he whispered.

'For what?'

'For anything. An engine perhaps, foghorn, ship's bell. All we've got's our ears and a compass. Thank God for the compass.'

'How long's it been like this?'

'A couple of hours maybe. We've had one near miss already, and one's enough. Get listening, Cessie, there's a girl.'

So I found myself a place at the gunwales. I scanned the impenetrable greyness around me, and listened, listened as hard as I could. But my ears, I discovered, were almost as useless as my eyes. All I could hear was the throb of our own engine and the sea running against the side of the boat.

The shape beside me moved and became Big Bethany. 'Can't be far now, Princessie,' she said, putting her arm round me. 'Can't be far.' Big Bethany mothered me, and everyone else, through the terrors of that night, a little word here, a little hug there.

It seemed as if we were entombed out there in the fog for hours. All the while the world was becoming lighter around us as the dawn filtered through the fog, but I could neither see any better nor hear any better. The harder I looked into it, the more fearsome were the shapes I began to imagine: a charging bull, a rearing dragon, a lion crouched and ready to pounce. Our shroud was a whiter shade of grey now, but it still felt like a shroud.

There was a shout from behind me. I turned. Harry was pointing out into the fog over the starboard side. 'There! There!' he cried. And even as he spoke there was a deafening blast of a foghorn, so thunderous, so close that we all looked now for the looming prow of a ship that must come out of the fog and run us down at any moment.

'Hang on! Hang on tight!' Popsicle called out, and the engines roared to full throttle. The boat surged forward underneath me. I clutched at Big Bethany and hung on to her. I saw Mary fall and go rolling over and over across the deck. Mac went after her, caught her and held her. Mary clung to him, sobbing. We didn't see it, until the last moment, a vast wall of a giant tanker, or a ferry perhaps, that passed astern of us by barely fifty metres and then vanished into the fog. I thought the danger was over, but it wasn't.

'Look out for the wash!' Popsicle stood now like the

lifeboatman on the model he'd made me, his feet apart, braced, fighting the wheel as the wash hit us broadside on and tossed us like a cork. It was as if we'd been suddenly thrown into the path of a raging typhoon.

I know I screamed – and I wasn't the only one. I could not stop myself. The sea crashed over the gunwales, smacking me in the chest and chilling me to the bone. Big Bethany clung on to me tight, and then we were suddenly out of it and into calmer water. I looked around me again. Popsicle was still at his wheel, and he was laughing out loud, wiping the water from his face.

'Look, you beggars, look what I see!' he cried. The fog ahead was wispy. It was thinning, it was quite definitely thinning. Moments later we saw a flashing light and the emerging shape of a lighthouse, and then a harbour wall. Popsicle throttled back. 'Dunkirk dead ahead,' he said. 'Dunkirk or I'm a Dutchman.'

I went over to be near him. 'Do you recognise it?' I asked. In the grey gloom of the dawn I could just make out a strand of beach stretching away into the murky distance.

'Not a thing,' Popsicle replied. 'I wouldn't, would I? It was a long time ago and, besides, the place was in ruins last time I saw it. But it's Dunkirk all right. If I plotted it right, Cessie, and I think I did – hope I did – then what you're looking at is Dunkirk town.'

As we entered the shelter of the harbour we left the last vestiges of the fog behind us. There was a solitary angler fishing from the harbour wall. He waved at us and we waved back. There didn't seem to be much happening in the harbour except for a couple of fishing boats unloading at the quayside. The fishermen stopped what they were doing and watched us come in. They were still watching us as we tied up behind them.

'*Magnifique*,' one of them called out. '*Le bateau, il est superbe, magnifique.*'

'*Bonjour*,' Harry shouted in reply, as Mac and Mary between them settled him in his wheelchair on the quayside. '*Allez la France!*' And the fishermen laughed and echoed it back at us.

'*Allez la France! Allez la France!*'

'What's that?' I asked.

'It's what they always shout at rugby matches,' said Harry. 'It's all the French I know – and *bonjour* of course.'

Once everyone was off the boat – and that took some while – Popsicle gathered us all together. 'If anyone asks,' he was saying, 'just remember we got lost, lost in the fog. We had to put in somewhere for safety. Blame it on the skipper if you like.' I looked out across the harbour towards the town. The streetlights were going off everywhere. It was almost daylight. But hardly a car was moving. There was still scarcely anyone about.

'Popsicle,' said Harry. 'That street where Lucie Alice lived, do you know where to find it?'

'There was a church just up the road from their house, I know that much. I used to hear the bells. That's all I remember. I'll ask. Someone'll be bound to know. I'll ask.'

So we all set off into town, Popsicle leading us, his photo of Lucie Alice in his hand. He asked and he asked. He asked everyone he met – a couple of dustbin-men, a postman, a motorist who had stopped at a red light. The response was always the same – first, a look of utter disbelief when they saw us coming, and then, when they'd had a look at Popsicle's photograph, a shrug and a shake of the head. No one seemed to recognise Lucie Alice – that didn't surprise me, it was obvious they were all too young to have known her – but none of them had heard of the Rue de la Paix either, and that did seem strange.

Mac shepherded us along the pavements, taking particular charge of Tweedledum and Tweedledee who seemed intent on stopping to look in every shop window. Whenever we had to cross a road, Mac was there to marshall us – at one point even holding up his hand to stop an approaching lorry, so that we could all cross over safely. But the further we walked the more exhausted we were all becoming, except Popsicle. Big Bethany had to sit down to catch her breath whenever she could. She had a wheezing cough that she kept apologising for. Now that a few of the shops were opening, Popsicle would dart in and show his photograph at every possible opportunity. We would stand and wait for him outside. It was hopeless. Every shake of the head, every shrug of the shoulders, told us so. But Popsicle never once lost heart.

He was walking on ahead up a narrow cobbled sidestreet, when he called for me to catch him up. He took my hand in his and squeezed it. 'The street where she lived, Cessie, it was like this, just like this. Little houses. Grey shutters. If I could find the church . . . I could hear church bells, Cessie, in my cupboard. And they were close, very close.' He wasn't looking at me at all as he spoke. 'The trouble is, Cessie, I'm beginning to wish I'd never started out on this whole caper. I'm thinking that maybe there's some things it's better not to know.'

I squeezed his hand back because it was all I could think to do. 'Popsicle!' It was Mac, calling from behind us. 'How about some breakfast? There's some of us could do with it. Warm us up. Army marches on its stomach, y'know.'

There was a café across the street. The lights were on inside. The door was open. A lady in a headscarf and a coat was sweeping the pavement outside vigorously. She saw us coming and stopped her sweeping. Like everyone else we'd met, I think she thought we were a bit strange at first, but as soon as she realised what we were after, she ushered us inside only too gladly.

With her coat and scarf off, she turned out to be a lot older than I had imagined. Not that she behaved old. She bustled about the place like a beaver, putting three tables together, arranging the chairs and talking nineteen to the dozen as she did so – all in French, so I didn't understand a word. When we had all finally sat down, she turned to Mac and said: 'English? *Anglais*?'

'Scots,' said Mac firmly, and she seemed puzzled by that.

'*Café*? Coffee? *Thé*? Breakfast?' she asked.

'Breakfast,' said Harry, patting his belly. 'Famished, we are.'

And so we found ourselves for the next hour or so thawing out in the warmth of the café, with baskets of freshly baked croissants and endless glasses of tea. No one wanted coffee. And Popsicle, I noticed, didn't want anything at all. He just sat there beside me staring down at the table, at the photograph of Lucie Alice, smoothing out the corners and saying nothing.

The old lady brought over yet more glasses of tea. 'You don't like it? The breakfast, it is not good?' she asked Popsicle. That was when Popsicle suddenly broke into French. It took us all by surprise, the old lady too. For a while it was difficult for me to understand what it was that they were talking about. Then Popsicle gave her the photograph and she looked at it closely. I began to recognise some of the words they were saying: 'Rue de la Paix' and 'Lucie Alice'. But that was all. After a while she spoke in English again – perhaps she hadn't entirely understood Popsicle's French. Perhaps it wasn't so good after all. 'You were here, in Dunkirk?' she said. 'In 1940?'

Popsicle nodded and turned the photo over in her hands. A long look passed between them.

'I have come to find her,' said Popsicle, speaking very slowly. '*Vous la connaissez*? You know Lucie Alice? Maillol, her last name was Maillol. You know where she is?' The old lady was studying the photograph closely, frowning at it. She took it to the door where the light was better. 'I can show my husband?' she said.

'Of course,' said Popsicle, and she hurried away out through the door at the back of the bar. We watched her go. It was Harry that broke the silence. 'I've just thought of something,' he said. 'Who's going to pay for this little lot? We haven't got any francs, have we? Didn't think of that, did you, Popsicle?'

But Popsicle wasn't listening to him. His eyes were fixed on the door behind the bar.

'She'll take pounds, won't she?' said Chalky. 'And if she won't, then we'll just have to get Benny to do the washing-up, won't we, Benny?' We were still laughing at that when she came back into the café. With her was an old man in a collarless shirt and braces. He was scrawny round the neck and unshaven. He had the photograph in his hand. He looked at us over the top of his glasses, suspicious, hostile almost. Popsicle got to his feet.

'You are the one who is looking for Lucie Alice Maillol?' the old man asked.

'Yes,' said Popsicle.

'Why? *Pourquoi*?'

'She's a friend. She saved my life. *Elle m'a aidé pendant la guerre. Elle m'a sauvé la vie.*'

I wasn't sure the old man understood. He came closer and looked up into Popsicle's face. 'She hid me,'

Popsicle went on. 'She hid me in her cupboard, in her house, in the Rue de la Paix.'

'But it is no longer there, *monsieur*. La Rue de la Paix, the old street, it is gone. How you say it? *Bombardée*. Destroyed. And Lucie Alice . . .'

'You know her?' Popsicle breathed.

'*Elle était dans la même école*, in the same school, *monsieur*, the same class. My wife, myself, Lucie Alice. We were friends, all of us. *Mais . . . nous sommes désolés, monsieur*. We are very sorry, but Lucie Alice, we have not seen her since 1940, since the war. No one has. One day, we go to see her, and she is gone. *Disparue. Sa mère aussi. Elles sont disparues toutes les deux.* Disappeared. They take them away. We never see them again.'

13 MESSAGE TO MY FATHER

POPSICLE FELT FOR THE CHAIR BEHIND HIM TO steady himself.

'You are sure?' he asked. 'You are quite sure?' The old man nodded as he handed back the photograph.

'Rue de la Paix, it is still there,' he said. 'They built it again after the war, like many other streets in Dunkirk. But Lucie Alice and her mother, we hear nothing of them ever again, nothing.'

Popsicle took a deep breath before he spoke again. 'I'll go for a walk, I think,' he said, more to himself than anyone else. 'Yes, I think I'll go for a little walk.' He tried to smile at us, but he couldn't do it. 'I won't be long. Why don't I meet you all back at the boat in a couple of hours? You'll see they're all there, won't you, Mac? Then we'll all go home.' And he was gone out of the door.

Harry put a hand on my arm. 'Best not leave him on his own, eh Princessie?' So I went after Popsicle and caught him up in the street.

'Where are we going?' I asked.

'Don't rightly know,' said Popsicle. 'Maybe we'll sit on the beach for a while, just for old time's sake. We can hardly come all this way for nothing, can we?' He took my hand and held on to it tight as if he needed me to be with him. I wanted to say something about Lucie Alice, something to comfort him, but I couldn't find the words. We walked on together in silence.

There were more people about in the streets now. We passed by the open door of a large baker's shop where they were busy stacking loaves and baguettes. The smell of them seemed to follow us down the street. 'Lovely,' I said, breathing it in. Popsicle hadn't heard me.

'Well,' he said. 'I suppose I got what I came looking for, didn't I? I wanted the truth and I got it. I wanted to know, and now I do. All I want now is to unknow it, if you see what I mean. But that's one thing you can never do, can you, Cessie?'

A bell rang out, loud and close by, a church bell. I stood there on the pavement and waited for it to finish. 'Eight o'clock,' I said. Popsicle was hurrying on without me. I ran after him.

'The bells, Cessie.' He grabbed my arm as I came alongside him. 'I know them. I know those bells.'

We turned into a small square with a fountain in the middle, and beyond it a huge, grey, stone church with gulls ranged along its rooftop.

We gazed up at the tower. 'They were the same bells,' said Popsicle, 'I'm sure of it. This is the church, it must be. Every Sunday she'd go to church, her and her mother. They'd leave me back in the house, shut up in my cupboard. I'd sit there in the dark and listen to those bells. I'd say a prayer or two for them, and for me too. Never been much of a churchgoing sort, not before, not since; but I prayed hard in that cupboard, Cessie, so hard. It doesn't seem like anyone was listening very much, does it?'

Popsicle was still trying to work out where the old Rue de la Paix might have been, when we saw a lady come into the square walking her dog. The dog looked just like Shirley Watson's dog back home – pop-eyed and snuffly and yappy. When he asked her for directions, the lady led us across the square and pointed to a narrow street that led down towards the sea. She was a lot more friendly than her dog. So at last we found the Rue de la Paix, and stood across the street from where Popsicle thought the house might have been.

'Nothing's the same. Different street, different house – except the shutters,' said Popsicle. 'The shutters were grey then too, grey and peeling. God, what a silly little beggar I was. I had to do it, didn't I? I had to open those shutters. I had to have a look out. The soldier who saw me, he must've been standing just about where we are now. Then they hauled me off that way, down towards the beaches. And that's the corner, that's where I saw Lucie Alice coming home with her bread. Oh, Cessie, what I'd give to see her come walking round that corner right now.'

We crossed the wide road that ran along the seafront, and walked along the beach. There was a chill breeze off the sea, so we went to sit down in the shelter of the dunes, where I discovered that French sand-hoppers were just the same as English ones, only there seemed to be more of them. The sea was murky grey and limpid. Each wave seemed so tired it barely had the strength to curl itself over and run up the sand. There were miles of beach, and miles of dunes, as far as the eye could see, all completely deserted, except for a couple of walkers out with their gambolling dogs.

Popsicle was looking out to sea. 'That young soldier,' he said, 'the one who pulled me out of the sea. I never even knew his name. I've still got that poetry book of his, *The Golden Treasury*, always kept it. Sitting here like this, Cessie, it's all so peaceful. You can hardly believe it happened, all those ships out there, and the planes screaming down on us, and the bombs, and the bodies. I remember walking away from him. He was a body, like the others, and I never even knew his name.'

'Names don't matter,' I said.

Popsicle seemed suddenly cheered by that. He put his arm round me and hugged me to him. 'That's a true fact, Cessie,' he said. 'That's a powerful fact. I may not know his name, but I have the memory of him, of what he did. Same with Lucie Alice. I'll never see her again, I know that now, but I have the memory of her, haven't I? And that's a whole lot better than nothing. If anyone should know that, then I should.'

He talked on and on, but I really didn't hear much of what he was saying. I was too cold, too tired to follow his thinking. After a while he seemed to sense it. 'Come on, Cessie,' he said, at last, helping me to my feet and brushing the sand off me. 'I'd better be getting you home. I'd better be getting us all home.'

We must have walked further than we thought – it seemed a very long way back to the harbour and the *Lucie Alice*. They were all on board and waiting for us, and so were the harbourmaster and the customs men.

Popsicle explained, in French and in English, how we'd got lost in the fog, that we had no passports, and that we were on our way home anyway. They complained a bit, and shrugged a lot, and then complained some more, but that was the end of it.

As we cast off there was a sense of deep sadness about the boat. They were clearly not at all the same cheery crew they had been. Even Harry had lost his sparkle and sat hunched and dejected in his wheelchair. I told him we'd been to the beaches. I told him about the sandhoppers, but he didn't seem to want to know. Big Bethany stood on her own, gazing back at Dunkirk. She had her handkerchief out and, because I knew why, I left her alone. Benny grumbled down in his galley, about all the washing-up he had to do. He didn't seem to want any help. Some of them had that vacant look on their faces, the same look I'd seen through the window up at Shangri-La.

I thought at first that it might be a kind of solidarity for Popsicle in his disappointment, but in that case you'd have thought they'd have been all over him with consideration and kindness, and they weren't. Then I thought they might be blaming him for bringing them on what had turned out to be a fool's errand, but that wasn't how they were, any of them. It wasn't only fatigue either, although that was evident on every face around me as we steamed out of Dunkirk harbour and into the swell of the open sea. As I was sitting on my own under the red ensign at the stern of the boat, I finally worked out what it was that must be making them all feel so wretched. It could be one of two things, or maybe both: an unspoken dread in each of them, the dread of going back to Shangri-La, or an aching sadness that their grand adventure, our grand adventure, would soon be over.

There had been an hour or so of this all-pervading gloom, when Popsicle called everyone together up on deck. He handed each of us a tin of condensed milk. 'To sweeten you up, you miserable beggars. Come on, it's not that bad. Do you think it's the last time we'll be doing this? Of course it's not. Don't you worry, I'll see to it.' He patted his wheel. 'We'll go out in the old girl whenever you want to. She's my boat, isn't she? I'll take her out whenever I want to. They can't stop us. Promise.'

They seemed to brighten a little at that. Popsicle hadn't finished. 'All right, so we didn't find what we came for. It didn't work out like I wanted. But we've had the time of our lives, haven't we? We may be a lot of old crocks, but I'm telling you, this old girl never had a finer crew, not even in her heyday. So let's not mope, eh? We'll scoff down our condensed milk, warm ourselves up with Benny's tea, and we'll all come home smiling. I want them to see us smiling. And they'll be waiting, you can be sure of that. There'll be quite a kerfuffle when we get back, I shouldn't wonder. And the Dragonwoman'll be there too, bound to be. So let's just show the old crow what a time we've had. Let's show her what we're made of. How about it?'

The first of the sun broke through and flooded the deck with sudden warmth. 'Here comes the sun,' cried Popsicle. 'Come on, Cessie. Get your fiddle out. Play us a tune, there's a girl.'

How Popsicle did it, I'll never know, but somehow he transformed all of us. Within minutes we were the same happy bunch we had been on the way over – well, almost. Popsicle said later it was the magical properties of condensed milk that did the trick. Whatever it was, it certainly wasn't my violin playing. I just couldn't get into my stride. My fingers wouldn't work as they should, and then my 'e' string broke and I didn't have a spare in my violin case. You can't play very much without an 'e' string.

'No matter,' said Popsicle. 'We'll have the radio instead. There'll be some music on. There always is.' He asked Mac to turn it on full volume so we could all hear it.

After a lot of wheezing and whistling and foreign-sounding stations, the radio at last settled on a clear signal, some jingly music, and then an English voice – a voice I knew at once, the voice of my father. Popsicle had recognised it too. He cut the engines at once.

'That's him!' he said. 'That's Arthur, that's my son! Listen, listen.'

'This then is a message to my father. I just hope and pray that you're listening out there, Popsicle.'

'He called you Popsicle,' I whispered.

'So he did, Cessie, so he did. Hush now and listen, there's a girl.' There was a pause so long that I thought the radio must have gone wrong. My father cleared his throat, and went on.

'All those years sitting on that wall I longed for you to come back. All my life ever since I've been wanting you to come home – that's the truth of it. And then when you did come, all I did was give you the cold shoulder and send you away again. What I did was shameful, I know that now; but just how shameful it was I never really understood until we found Cessie gone this morning, until we read your letter, Cessie, the one you threw away. Lowestoft, the *Michael Hardy*, Dunkirk, Lucie Alice, my mother – I know it all now, I know you've gone off to look for Lucie Alice in Dunkirk.

I pray you find her alive and well, but if you do not, then please come home and be with us. We want you with us. I want you with me. There'll be no more Shangri-La, I promise you that. And, Cessie, if you're listening out there, come home safe and sound and bring Popsicle with you. Take care, both of you.' I thought he'd finished, but he hadn't, not quite. 'I've played a lot of requests on my shows over the years, but this is the first one I've ever requested myself. This is for you, Popsicle, to serenade you home. I know you're a lot older than sixty-four, but it'll have to do. Here it is then: "When I'm Sixty-four" by the Beatles. God bless. We'll be waiting for you.'

Those who knew it – and that was most of us – hummed or sang or clapped along. But Popsicle stood at his wheel and just listened, gazing out to sea all the while. When it had finished, he rubbed his hands together and blew on them. 'Cold. It's cold out here,' he said. 'Let's go home, shall we, Cessie?' And he started up the engines.

As Popsicle had predicted, there was indeed quite a reception committee waiting for us. In mid-Channel a helicopter found us and circled overhead for a while. We were still several kilometres off when the first boat came out to meet us, a police launch. They came alongside and, through a loudhailer, offered to put a couple of officers on board – to help us, they said. Popsicle refused, and made it very plain that we were quite capable of bringing the *Lucie Alice* in under her own steam and needed no help whatsoever. They seemed a bit disgruntled at that and told us rather curtly to follow them in. Popsicle replied that we were a lot bigger than they were and faster too, so they could follow us – if they could keep up, that is.

Word had clearly got about, because before long there was a flotilla of small ships all around us escorting us in. The closer we came to the shore, the more there were. Another helicopter was hovering overhead now. There was a cameraman on board, hanging out of the side as he filmed us. It was as if we'd been single-handed round the world, not just over to Dunkirk and back.

Once inside the harbour there was a cacophony of hooting all around us, and one ship had even turned on its fire hoses to greet us. The quay was lined with people cheering and waving. My arms were aching with waving back; but I never stopped, not once. Popsicle stayed at the helm, as he had done all the way. I looked up at him and I could see that, tired though he was, he was enjoying every moment of it, as I was, as were all the ancient Argonauts. You may not have brought back your Golden Fleece, Jason Popsicle, I thought, but even if you had, the welcome could not possibly have been any better.

We were edging our way back into the lock when I first saw my father and my mother. They were standing side by side in front of the lock-keeper's house, slightly apart from the rest of the crowd, as if they wanted to enjoy it all by themselves, in private.

It seemed an age before we were through the lock and tied up once again, the great engines silent at last. I saw Chalky give them a last wipe, and kissing each of them a fond goodbye. Big Bethany enveloped me against her warm softness and said I was to come and play my violin for them one day up at Shangri-La. I promised, and I meant it too.

My mother was first on board. It was while we were still clinging to each other that I saw Shirley Watson and Mandy Bethel, and a few others besides, watching from the towpath. I wriggled my fingers at them. They wriggled theirs back. After a time I managed to disengage from my mother. My father was looking at his father.

'We heard you, Arthur, on the radio,' Popsicle said.

'Welcome home, Popsicle,' said my father. And there on the deck of the *Lucie Alice* they hugged each other, for all the world to see; and judging from the applause, all the world seemed to be enjoying it hugely. They hugged and hugged, long enough, I thought – and I hoped – to make up for all the years they hadn't.

Which type of book do you like best?

Take the quiz . . . then read the book!

Who would you like to have an adventure with?
a) On my own
b) A ghost
c) Someone in my family
d) My best friend
e) My pet

Where would you like to go on holiday?
a) A remote island or a far-away mountain
b) A fantasy world
c) Anywhere as long as my family and friends are there
d) A different time period
e) The countryside

I would like to be . . .
a) Explorer
b) Author
c) Someone who helps others
d) Warrior
e) Circus ringmaster

My favourite stories are . . .
a) Full of adventure
b) Magical
c) About friendships and family
d) War stories
e) About animals

If you answered mostly with A you'll enjoy . . .

KENSUKE'S KINGDOM

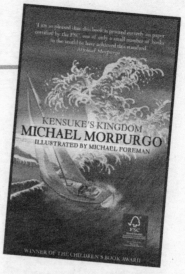

Washed up on an island with no food and water, Michael cannot survive. But he is not alone . . .

If you answered mostly with B you'll enjoy . . .

THE GHOST OF GRANIA O'MALLEY

There is gold in the Big Hill, but Jessie and Jake can't bear for the hill to be destroyed. Can they save it before it's too late?

If you answered mostly with C you'll enjoy . . .

LONG WAY HOME

George doesn't want to spend his summer with another foster family . . . but this time he may have found somewhere to call home.

If you answered mostly with D you'll enjoy . . .

FRIEND OR FOE

It is the Blitz. One night David and his friend see a German plane crash on the moors. Do they leave the airmen to die?

If you answered mostly with E you'll enjoy . . .

WAR HORSE

In the deadly chaos of the
First World War, one horse
witnesses the reality of
battle from both sides
of the trenches.

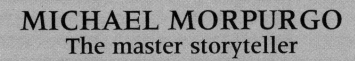

MICHAEL MORPURGO
The master storyteller

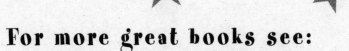

EGMONT PRESS: ETHICAL PUBLISHING

Egmont Press is about turning writers into successful authors and children into passionate readers – producing books that enrich and entertain. As a responsible children's publisher, we go even further, considering the world in which our consumers are growing up.

Safety First
Naturally, all of our books meet legal safety requirements. But we go further than this; every book with play value is tested to the highest standards – if it fails, it's back to the drawing-board.

Made Fairly
We are working to ensure that the workers involved in our supply chain – the people that make our books – are treated with fairness and respect.

Responsible Forestry
We are committed to ensuring all our papers come from environmentally and socially responsible forest sources.

**For more information, please visit our website at
www.egmont.co.uk/ethical**

MIX
Paper
FSC FSC® C018306